BADLANDS BORN

WADE PETERSON

For Colleen

1

Jasmine's eyes opened to a chipboard ceiling with a scream echoing in her ears. A sunbeam fell through a small hazy window, over faded gray and brown floorboards, a scarred table, and two wooden chairs. Dust motes chased each other in and out of the shadows. Asphalt and mildew tugged at her memory, and she felt her last memories slip away.

She pushed herself to her elbows, head clear, free of pain for the first time since she couldn't remember. No pain at all, not even the little aches and strains that had become constant companions over the year. Her joints moved smoothly, without a single creak or pop. Her mind felt clear and nimble, like she'd had a triple espresso – without the jitters. Was she sleeping? She pinched herself.

Ouch.

Okay, not sleeping. Just stuck in a musty shack. Except, as she looked around, she remembered the place. Her brother Ryan had taken the table from the garage, she had pulled the chairs from the basement, the mirror on the wall was stolen from a neighbor's garage sale, and a footlocker in the corner was Ryan's own. He had wanted something to store all their secret kids' stuff from the adult's snooping. The asphalt smell was the roof's leaky tarpaper that couldn't keep all the rain out. As kids, they hadn't cared about the damp and mildew, she even thought it made the place more fun because it kept the adults away. She hadn't been here in decades.

Dad had torn the treehouse down when they were thirteen.

Someone had painted slogans on the far wall. She recognized the first, a crossed out NO GIRLS ALLOWED, Ryan's failed attempt to claim the treehouse for himself. The others she didn't remember.

WELCOME BACK
YOU'RE OK
FOLLOW THE LIGHTS TO PARADISE
BEWARE THE BLOOD WEEPER
DON'T FUCK IT UP THIS TIME

All the messages were in Ryan's hand, which was odd considering he had died seventeen years ago. As she looked closer, there was a black spot under the list where letters suggested themselves beneath a hasty paint job. She knelt closer and made out the original message.

TRUST BISHOP

She stood and scratched at a tingling inside her elbow. Had Ryan painted these messages and finally pushed Dad to tear this place down? Her brother always did have a weird sense of humor. She walked around, letting her fingers fall over the familiar scars on the chairs and tabletop. The window's scratched, dirty glass didn't let in anything other than sunlight and hint at dark shapes just outside swaying in the breeze. Her stomach rumbled. She would let it wait. One thing life taught her was filling an empty stomach could wait, the food never tasted as good as you thought it would. Still, she couldn't put it off forever.

She passed the mirror and stopped. The face was hers, but hadn't been for a while. Her long-lost cheekbones were back. Her dark hair was long, straight, and shiny, but pulled back in a ponytail. And were those bangs? She reached up. Sure enough, held in place with hairspray. She looked down and found herself wearing a red polo, white shorts, and white Keds with no socks. When had she last dressed like this? She had dropped the preppy look after Ryan had...

She scratched at her elbow again. This was all wrong; she wasn't the little Japanese girl trying to fit in with the blonde WASPs anymore. The treehouse certainly hadn't been around when she was a teenager, and it now seemed smaller than before. She couldn't breathe.

"Settle down," she said. "Trapdoor. Think, Jas, where was it?"

The floorboards ran uninterrupted from wall to wall. She turned over the table, moved the footlocker, but couldn't find the door. The window. She gripped a chair by its legs and swung, glass shattering with a sound like little bells. The chair cracked and tumbled to the floor, leaving a split leg in her hand.

It's got a point on it. Probably could drive it right into the heart. Though if you miss, you'd probably just puncture a lung or get a nasty infection.

She shook her head and let the leg clatter to the floor. The window, apart from a hand-sized piece still lodged in the corner, was big enough to shimmy through. She reached for the glass and jerked back as her thumb caught an edge. She sucked at it for a bit before looking. Blood flowed from a slash about an inch long, and she felt her stomach flutter.

One slash, and it's all over. Gotta do it quick before the blood makes it slippery.

The blood streamed around her palm and pattered to the floor. Bloody fingerprints dotted the glass, and bile rose in her throat. She closed her eyes and threw the glass away.

Coward. You're just so useless.

Her eyes welled.

You going to cry, Jas? Typical.

∼

SHE DIDN'T KNOW how long she stayed on the floor, rocking and shaking and sobbing. Eventually she stopped and rubbed her burning eyes. Her shirt was starting to stick to her back. She looked at her shorts, which had a rusty brown spot where she had pressed her thumb to stop the bleeding. Just another thing she had ruined.

She walked to the footlocker, and opened it. She expected to find the toys, notebooks, or the old bird's nest they stored as kids but only found a framed family portrait. Dad wore a polo and jeans. Mom, not a speck of gray in her hair, in a sundress. Ryan wore his habitual acid-wash jean jacket and concert tee, long hair pulled behind his left ear to feature the stud he had put in weeks before. And there she was, hair in a ponytail, red polo, white shorts, and Keds. The same outfit she wore now. There was something about the picture she was forgetting. She reached down to touch the frame, then thought better of it and closed the footlocker's lid and turned to the window. She hated that picture.

She really was in a tree, with a clear sky showing through brown leaves.

She got up and walked to the window, stepping around the broken chair and avoiding the glass. The air was a little cooler outside; she had forgotten how stuffy the tree house could get. The ground looked to be about ten feet away: dry brown grass and packed dirt with few rocks. She looked back over her shoulder at the writing on the wall.

FOLLOW THE LIGHTS TO PARADISE

"We'll try it your way, Ryan," she said.

On the ground, she found herself in a clearing. The trees, apart from the one supporting the tree house, were scrawny things with withered yellow leaves. Over the treetops to her left, she saw a ribbon of deep red rock jutting out into the sky. High, thin clouds curled overhead, as if they were soap bubbles being pulled toward some far-away drain.

Jasmine walked through the forest toward the red rocks, picking her way between exposed tree roots and deadfalls. Dry leaves rasped as the wind whipped them around and a crow called out somewhere in the distance, but otherwise the forest was silent. Given the yellow and brown grasses and dying trees, Jasmine could hardly imagine songbirds or insects surviving in this place.

She stared at the ground and put one foot in front of the other, only glancing up to see if she was still heading more or less toward the red rocks. Her stomach rumbled. It figures she would lose weight just in time to starve. But that's okay, she reminded herself, she would probably die of dehydration first. That looks like what did in everything else.

The woods and brush gave way to a road. Unlike the woods, the asphalt looked like it had just been put down yesterday. The blacktop was so black and smooth, it reflected the colors of the trees like a pond. Bright white lines ran down each edge. A dashed canary-yellow centerline glowed against the asphalt with no trace of tire tread having ever crossed it. Crushed red gravel lined the shoulders, apparently made from the same rock as the ridge in the distance. The road went on in both directions as far as she could see. No signs, no hints as to where they led.

"Oh hell," she said.

She sat down, brought her knees to her chin, and closed her eyes. This isn't fair, she thought. God was punishing her. She'd die here by the side of the road, and no one would care. Worse, maybe God wouldn't let her die and she'd be stuck wandering around forever, always hungry, always thirsty.

Something tickled at the edge of her hearing. It sounded like music—a guitar. She cocked her head and concentrated. She could just pick out the occasional high notes as the music faded and came back on the breeze. Her heart rose and she let out a breath. She wasn't alone anymore.

Maybe they knew where to get some food and water, she thought. They may even know exactly what this place was. Still, she hesitated. If she had to follow the lights to paradise, then maybe she wasn't there yet. Ryan wrote about a blood weeper; he once trusted someone named Bishop, then decided against it. Maybe she was safer on her own.

The music stopped, leaving Jasmine with only the sound of dry leaves on the wind, alone again. She jumped up and ran down the road. She'd be careful, she told herself.

2

Jasmine tried ignoring the pains in her stomach, both those caused by the rocks she lay on and those from hunger. In his camp, the guitar player sat on the ground in the shadow of a massive dead tree. His car, a silver sedan from the sixties or seventies, was losing the battle with rust. The man looked like a roadie from a rock concert, with a lanky build, black stingy hair, and dark gold-rimmed sunglasses. A black t-shirt, black jeans with a silver wallet chain, and black Chuck Taylor high-top sneakers completed the look.

The man played something vaguely bluesy, mostly rock. Jasmine couldn't recognize it. Lots of power chords though, like the music Ryan had liked. She liked to tell her brother power chords and amplifiers were crutches for the musically stupid, when she wanted to get under his skin. But this man played well for all his atrocious taste, she supposed, his fingers never fumbling when changing chords or during bridge pieces that sent his fingers all over the fret board like a dancing centipede. And he had food.

A can of beans or maybe stew sat next to a small fire. The wind would tease her, bringing the smell to her, then taking it away as her stomach grumbled. Between songs the man would stop and give the can a stir, taking a taste. She tried to summon up the courage to go out and ask for some food but couldn't. Perhaps it was the oddness of being a teenager again, or the warnings in the tree house, or maybe it was because the guitar player wore a pistol on one hip, a machete on the other, and had a rifle leaning against the tree behind him.

Finally after playing something Jasmine could almost name, the man tasted the beans and put his instrument aside.

He ate slowly, blowing on each spoonful before he put it in his mouth. Jasmine thought about running away and hiding until later, but the man was staring right at her hiding spot and would see her if she moved. She closed her eyes and hoped her stomach wouldn't give her away.

The can dropped to the ground, and footsteps crunched on gravel. She looked up and saw the man slide his guitar into the sedan's back seat. He looked over his shoulder—was he looking right at her? No, she was too well hidden. He slid behind the wheel and the engine roared to life, a smooth throaty growl hinting at greater power. She half expected him to rev it a few times like a kid in high school (it was something Ryan would have done), but the man put the car in gear and backed out onto the road. He drove slowly and looked back once more in her direction. She stayed put. He drove like that for a few hundred feet at a parade pace before he gunned the engine and the silver car roared down the road.

In a few moments, the car rounded a corner and drove from sight. She waited until the engine's echoes died out before she moved.

Her heart raced as she broke into the open, and her hands shook as she reached for the can, dented with reddish dirt smudged along its lip. It was empty—mostly empty, she corrected herself. Bits of vegetables and meat stuck to the sides. Her mouth watered. She walked back to the tree with the can, fishing the remnants out with a finger.

"Great, Jas, you're too scared to ask for help, so it's leftovers." She popped a carrot bit into her mouth, savoring the spicy, meaty gravy that coated it. Her teeth crunched on something hard. "And dirt." She peered closer and tried to find bits not covered in red dust but gave up when she realized her hands were coated in the stuff anyway. She used her cleanest finger to fish out a potato morsel.

"In fact," she said, digging at the bottom for the last drops of gravy, "This place pretty much sucks. Next time, just—ouch!"

Her finger came away bleeding. A drop welled and fell against the tree. "Just great." She sucked at the finger and kept it in her mouth while she looked for something to stop the blood. The guy with the guitar probably had a first aid kit in his car. She pinched the cut closed and waited until the bleeding slowed down to an ooze. She wiped the blood against the tree and went back to the can, tipping it and trying to navigate the last drop of gravy past the dirt-crusted spots into her mouth.

～

THE CAN, emptied of its last possible morsel, sat at her feet. The sun set blood-red on the horizon, and the red stone hills cast long shadows across the highway. Jasmine wrapped her arms around herself. The fire was down to coals, and she mentally slapped herself for not thinking to look for more firewood when the light was better. Add that to the list along with no food, water, or idea of what to do next, she thought.

She watched the red sun fall behind the hill. She figured she had about fifteen minutes of light left, maybe twenty. She leaned back against the tree and closed her eyes. The tree relaxed her, almost like a massage chair. It must be something in the wind, she thought, something making it sway rhythmically, sending a throbbing through her back. A pulse, like a heartbeat, ran from the base of her spine through her head. Then the branches groaned, and the tree's pulse thumped faster.

Her eyes flew open. She could feel the thrum-thrum of its pulse through the soles of her feet, and the branches rustled above her. She stumbled back as the tree started quivering. A fresh cool breeze blew, bringing with it the smells of spring. The branches swelled and blisters formed at the tips. No, not blisters, she realized, buds. Tiny buds appeared over all the branches of the forty-foot tree, then burst into little green leaves. The leaves unfurled, blotting out the red-and-orange sky above. The thrumming faded, and the oak swayed in the breeze, the leaves a soothing whisper to her. She stared up at it, fixed by its beauty.

She lay down beneath the oak and gazed into the branches until her eyes drooped, feeling safer under its leaves than the open sky. The fire had died out completely, and she shivered in the cool air. How could it be so damn hot during the day and freezing at night? Her stomach growled again. It just wasn't fair.

She shifted around, trying to get comfortable. She knew something wasn't right with this place, but she was too tired to do anything about it right now. With any luck she would know more tomorrow.

. . .

SHE WOKE to the sound of shuffling feet. A kind of drag-step, shuffle-step.

"Hello?" she said. The shuffling stopped for a moment, then started again. A dark shadow swayed twenty feet away, between her and the woods. There wasn't much light, just enough to make out a person-shaped outline.

Drag-step, shuffle-step.

"Hello?" The figure kept coming. Then she smelled it, like a walking pit toilet. Jasmine stood as it approached, feeling her body's need to run but staring at the figure approaching with its drag-step, shuffle-step.

Then it whispered.

"Hahhhh-sssss. Hahhh-ssss."

"Go away," she said.

"Hahhh-sss." It reached for her. Drag-step, shuffle-step. Fingers grasped and released greedily.

Jasmine's paralysis disappeared. She threw the closest thing at hand—the empty stew can—at the figure. The can bounced off its head without any visible effect. Jasmine jumped up and ran toward the road. Her feet found the centerline, and then she was caught in a wall of light and screeching tires. She threw her hands out, and the light swung away, coming to center on the thing behind her: a man dressed in rags, hairless but for a few tufts scattered around his scalp. The skin on his face sagged as if the bones and muscle beneath had melted. Open sores and scabs pocked the face, arms, and legs. But what chilled Jasmine most was the eyes. They stared blankly, without intelligence or emotion.

When the headlights caught him full-on, he threw a thin arm over his eyes and turned his head before folding under the car with a wet crunch. Jasmine fell to her knees, feeling the pavement's warmth seep into her. The car door opened and man with the guitar ran to her, holding a machete.

"Are there any more?" he asked.

She shook her head, still staring at the place where the man had disappeared under the car.

"You hurt?"

She shook her head again. "No, I don't think so." Her voice shook a little, but she was proud that her voice worked at all. "Was that a—"

"Deader, yeah." He pulled her to her feet. "Come on, there may be more."

"Was he dead like me?" she asked, letting herself be pulled to the car. The hood was spattered with something dark. A foot twitched just under the front tires. The man turned her head away and pushed her gently but firmly into the front seat.

"Not exactly," he said.

He pulled a blanket from the back seat, which he wrapped around her.

"Is this heaven?" she asked as he slid into the driver's seat.

"I sure as hell hope not." He put the car in gear, and they drove away into the night.

3

———————

Jasmine woke with the sun in her eyes. Her neck and back screamed their protest at having been in one position for too long, and her head pounded like she had been drinking all night. They were driving along the pristine highway; dead trees and red rock hills passed on either side.

"You up?" the man said. He drove with one hand on the red steering wheel, the opposite arm propped up against his window, like he was lounging in an evening chair.

A sarcastic retort died on her lips as her eyes saw the blood on the hood. Bile rose in her throat. Red dashboard, upholstered red seats, red carpeting under her feet. She was swimming in blood.

"Pull over," she said.

"Huh?"

"Gotta—" She retched but managed to keep everything down. The man cursed as he pulled to the shoulder. Jasmine fumbled at the handle and got the door half-open before she vomited on the gravel shoulder at thirty miles an hour. The car came to a stop as the last of her precious meal left her.

"You okay?" he asked.

Jasmine shook her head and pointed blindly at the hood. "That."

"What?"

"That is still on the hood. From last night."

"Yeah, can't do much about it right now. Maybe later."

Jasmine spat the sour bits from her mouth and closed the door. Red, it's just a color, right? Pull it together, Jas.

"It's okay, I'll be okay. Just wasn't expecting it."

The man reached into the back seat and brought out a canteen.

"Water," he said, "not a lot of this around. Swish it around, swallow it. Got it?"

Jasmine nodded and poured a capful into her mouth. It had a bitter taste, like concentrated pool water. She swished and swallowed anyway. The man nodded and pulled back on the road.

"Thanks," she said.

"Think you can keep it down from now on? You hurl inside the Biscayne here and we got problems."

Jasmine nodded and looked out her window to avoid the gristly paint job on the hood.

"Am I really dead?" she asked.

"I don't know. You're breathing, your heart's beating. Are you dead?"

"Are you?"

He smiled. "Very much alive."

"I thought heaven would be different."

"I imagine it is."

"So I'm in hell." But that couldn't be right, she didn't believe in hell.

"Don't know about that either. We call this place the Badlands."

"That guy you ran over. Would he have really killed me?"

"Sure as you're made of meat."

Jasmine shuddered. She focused on the hills going by, dirt mounds with exposed faces of blood-red rock, like a giant had slashed the earth and left it to bleed.

"What'd you call him, a deader?"

"Yeah. Thank God it was just the one."

"How many are there?"

"I don't know, too damn many. Always come running once they get the scent."

"The scent of what?"

"Food, water, blood—especially blood. They're like sharks that way."

"But he looked human." Jasmine felt the man's gaze on the back of her neck.

"It was, once. It ain't anymore."

"So what are they?"

"Badlands cursed. You go hungry out here, you don't exactly die, you turn into one of them. Your heart stops, you breathe air, but you don't need it, and your mind dies. All you are is a stomach with legs."

Jasmine closed her eyes. She needed someplace safe until she could find her brother, or Jesus. She needed food and water too. She didn't know squat about heaven. She would need someone to teach her. This guy wasn't her first choice for a guide, but she wasn't in a position to choose. Might as well be friendly.

"My name's Jasmine."

"Yeah, I know."

She flinched and turned to face him. "What?"

"You're prettier than your picture."

"What?"

He fished out a wallet from his back pocket, pulled out a cracked photo, and handed it to her. It was a wallet-sized version of the picture from the tree-house. "Where'd you get this?"

"Your brother gave it to me."

A memory snapped into place. Mom flipping through pictures just back from the drugstore, her trembling hands setting the family picture aside. "But this picture didn't come back until after the funeral. Where'd he get it?"

"I don't know."

"You knew him?" she asked.

His face darkened. "Used to. He was here when we all woke up."

"We?"

"Everyone. The whole Badlands. My first memory is brushing the sand off myself and there he was, handing me a beer."

She absorbed that idea, or tried to.

Focus, Jas, he said he used *to know Ryan.*

"Is he dead?"

"I fucking doubt it."

She thought about dropping the matter. But then again, how could she find him if she didn't ask?

"Where is he?" she asked.

"Hopefully somewhere where he can't fuck things up any worse."

Ryan's instructions on the wall came back to her.

DON'T FUCK IT UP THIS TIME

Jasmine didn't say anything for a mile or two. The man drove without comment or any apparent concern for her. He hummed a tune under his breath while brown scrub brush, rocks, and dirt passed by her window.

"Why'd you come back?" she asked. "To the tree, I mean."

"No one deserves to be eaten by a deader, not even Ryan's sister."

"Well, thanks, uh ..."

"Bishop." He stuck out his hand.

Jasmine hesitated.

"Ah, I see you've heard of me," Bishop said. He held out the hand a few moments longer until it was obvious Jasmine wasn't going to shake it. "For someone who just got her sweet ass saved by yours truly, you could be a touch friendlier."

"I was warned," she said.

"What did you hear? That I'll steal your stuff? Sell you in chains? Try and get in your pants?"

Jasmine shook her head.

"Don't let the hype get to you, Jasmine, I'm not so bad. I'm not a thief or a slaver."

She stared at him. He gave her a grin.

"Oh don't worry, I'll keep my hands to myself too, if you like." He lowered his dark shades and met her eyes. Whatever effect it was supposed to have on her was ruined by the leer.

"Yeah, let's try it that way," she said.

Bishop shrugged.

"Don't know what you're missing. Any rumors you heard about me in the sack are *true*."

"Uh-huh," Jasmine said and went back to looking out her window.

They continued in silence down the road for several miles. Her stomach gurgled.

"I'm hungry," she said.

"There are lima beans in the back."

"What about that stew you had yesterday?"

"In the trunk."

"Well stop and let's get some out."

"Nope. We aren't stopping until later."

"I hate lima beans."

"Then I guess we don't have anything to eat then, do we?"

His smug tone made her want to slap him. Her stomach needed something, but damned if she was going to eat lima beans.

"I guess not," she said.

She studied Bishop's side of the car, which showed considerably more wear than hers. A Navajo-patterned blanket covered yellowed foam sprouting from split upholstery. The rough texture of the dashboard had worn smooth on either side of the steering wheel. The door panel's holes exposed the inner workings of the window and door latch. A machete was slung alongside the seat, its brass-riveted wood handle banging against his knee. She didn't want to know how often he had to use it.

The dashboard was all dials and needles, blocky numbers with squared-off zeroes. The dash itself was molded plastic that would split her skull quite nicely when her seat belt failed. The vents were jammed fully open, handles broken, air streams all aimed at Bishop. She claimed her side's vents and turned them her way. Not that it did any good; she was still hot. She looked again at Bishop, but he stared straight ahead, unreadable behind the gold-rimmed aviators.

The only thing not original to the dash was the stereo. It seemed shoe-horned into place, all black plastic with a little slot for a cassette. A chintzy plastic contraption hung underneath the radio, holding several naked cassette tapes whose lettering had worn away in the middle.

"Is there anything to read?" Jasmine said.

"Try the glove compartment," Bishop said.

Jasmine opened the box and saw a yellow cover peeking out behind some crushed beer cans. She pulled out a thick book titled *Owner's Manual: 1966 Chevy Biscayne*.

"You've got to be kidding," Jasmine said.

"I might have a titty mag in the back seat."

"Forget it."

"That radio work?" she asked.

"Last time I checked."

"Can we listen to something?"

Bishop reached over and pushed a button. Over-produced guitar chords backed by tinny synthesized trumpets and booming bass drum blared from the speakers. The singer wailed about a final countdown, though he never seemed to specify what the countdown was for, or what made it final.

"Is there anything else?"

Bishop shrugged; a finger on the steering wheel tapped in time with the beat. "It's the only station I know of."

"Is it all like this?"

"Sometimes they play Run DMC."

She shook her head. "No, I mean isn't there something else like classical?"

"You mean AC/DC?"

"Ugh." Jasmine reached out to the tapes. "What's in here?"

Bishop's slap struck like a rattlesnake.

"Ow!" She rubbed at her hand.

"Leave those alone," he said. "I have each one just where I want them, and I don't need you screwing it up."

She sat back in the seat and folded her arms.

"Stuck on a road trip in a Detroit death trap, zombies in the wilderness, nothing to eat but lima beans, and eighties music on the radio. I *am* in hell."

Bishop tilted his head back and roared in laughter.

LATER IN THE DAY, a small flat-topped building came into view as they rounded a curve. Bishop slowed down.

"You still hungry?" Bishop asked, bringing the car to a stop.

"Yes." Her stomach gurgled in agreement.

"Good. You know how to use a gun?"

"I don't like guns."

"Duly noted." He reached behind the seat and brought out a shotgun.

"This is the simplest one I have. Put the stock here tight against your shoulder, point the other end at anything that drools or points a gun at you, and pull the trigger."

"I'm not shooting this," she said.

He talked right over her. "Then you pull this part on the bottom all the way toward you, and it'll spit out the spent shell. Then slide it back to the front and it loads the next shell. Now you're ready to shoot the next thing that moves, unless it's me."

"No."

Bishop grabbed her by the shoulders. The wise-ass lecher had disappeared, replaced with something quiet and brutal.

"Let me put it to you this way. You are riding in my car, drinking my water, and eating my food. If you want to keep on doing that, you gotta carry your own weight. You will carry this gun and shoot anyone and anything trying to kill us, understand?"

"But I don't want to kill anyone."

"Do you want them to kill you?"

"No."

"Then pull the damn trigger when the time comes."

He put the gun in her hand, heavy and smelling of metal and oil. He left the car, slinging a rifle over his shoulder and pulling the machete free of its sheath.

"Come on, babe, let's go shopping."

They parked the Biscayne under a signpost with three glass globes. On each yellow globe a single word had been painted in red: FOOD, BEER, ICE.

"It's Curdy's Grocery," Jasmine said.

"Who?"

"It's a store we used to have outside of town. They tore it down years ago after the Walmart came in," Jasmine said. "But now it's here."

"It's just a food dump. They're the same all over the Badlands."

"There are more?"

"A few. They used to be all around here. Wherever you were having a party, there would always be one of these around, stocked to the roof with exactly what you needed."

"Who built them?"

"Your brother." He walked to the entrance.

Inside, the place was filled with rusted carts, empty shelves, and overturned registers. Jasmine walked behind Bishop through a carpet of candy wrappers and cardboard boxes. Sunlight came in through the broken windows around the perimeter, forcing shadows to huddle in the middle. In one aisle, someone had once started a campfire. Ash and charred bits of wood were heaped inside a ring of tin cans filled with dirt. Part of the floor warped beneath a creosote-stained hole in the ceiling.

"Are you sure there's food in here?"

"Maybe not, but we can use other things besides food. Look for anything that's intact, I don't care what it is. We'll take it outside and sort through it when we're done."

They shuffled through the aisles, Bishop in front poking with his machete, Jasmine behind, walking where Bishop had stepped and keeping the shotgun pointed behind them. They walked in silence, apart from the whistling wind and the crunching of feet on debris. Every so often, Bishop would stop to pick up a dented can. Sometimes after shaking it, he threw it away. Otherwise, he would smell it, tossing it if it smelled of rust or decay. Only if it had passed all the tests would he put it into a rucksack.

The clash between the Curdy's of her memories and her current surroundings reached a new height in the meat department. Jasmine remembered the rows of beef, poultry, and pork under a smiling cartoon cow, chicken, and pig painted on the back wall. In this store only the outlines of the cartoons remained, and the cuts of meat below them had all turned into black gelatinous mounds on plastic-wrapped foam trays. The smell was of dried death, not overwhelming, but the putrid vapors filled her nose each time she rounded an aisle.

"I would hate to have been in here when that stuff turned rotten," Jasmine said.

"It was a bad scene. But it's worse now. Maybe the meat was rotten then, but people still had hope your brother would come and fix all this."

"You make it sound like he was God or something."

"For some of us, he was. Hello—"

Bishop stooped and picked up a box of dishwasher detergent.

"Let me guess, you have a load of dishes just waiting for some soap?" Jasmine said.

Bishop smiled and put the box into his rucksack.

"How was my brother God? I lived with him his whole life, and he couldn't even make mac and cheese."

"If he wanted something, it would just happen. These stores always appeared when he showed up for a party. If someone told him the shelves had been all cleaned out, he'd be like 'no they aren't' and damn if they weren't all full up again."

"That doesn't make him God."

"You don't understand," Bishop said. "He made everything here, not just the food dumps, but the buildings, the cars, the cycles, the guns, the fucking road, Jas. Before him, none of this was here."

"What about the people? What did you do before he came?"

Bishop looked away and began poking through the rubbish.

Jasmine shook her head. "My brother was never into details. How could he think up an entire world? Could there have been something or someone that came before Ryan?"

Bishop shrugged. "Possibly. But if anyone was here before him, there's no trace of 'em."

Jasmine sighed. "Okay, fine." She thought for a moment. "But what happened if the food ran out?"

"They invited your brother to a party, that's what. Eventually, he was on a kind of regular route, stopping at a different party every night. I drove him everywhere."

"But he left."

"Yeah, he left."

Out by the Biscayne, they looked over their haul. One can of refried beans, half a pouch of powdered milk that didn't look moldy, a tube of tomato paste, a can of cat food, floor cleaner, and the box of dishwasher soap.

"Not a bad haul. We should be set for the rest of the week."

"Week?" Jasmine said. "There's not enough here for one person, unless you can live off of floor cleaner. I—"

Bishop held up a hand and cocked an ear.

"What? I don't hear anything."

"Shh!"

Jasmine listened. The wind picked up, and she heard an engine droning. It pitched up, like someone accelerating.

"Is that a motorcycle?" she asked.

It echoed through the canyons. She couldn't tell if it was getting closer.

"Toss that in the back seat," Bishop said, pointing at the cans and boxes "We've got trouble."

"What is it?" she asked, but Bishop was already running to the Biscayne.

She gathered up the cans and ran after him. She threw the things into the back and tumbled into her seat as Bishop accelerated out of the parking lot. Her door swung shut, slamming into her knee.

"Ow! What the hell, Bishop? It's just a guy on a motorcycle."

Bishop shook his head.

"I know that cycle. The dude who rides it ain't no one you want to meet. They call him the Blood Weeper."

Metal flashed over the rise. Bishop sat straighter in his seat. Jasmine looked over the dash at the approaching motorcycle.

"Get down," Bishop said.

"Why?" Jasmine said. "Ow!"

He pinned her head to the seat, holding it there with his hand.

"Do as I say, little girl, if you want to live."

"I'm not a little girl!"

"Don't squirm. If he thinks it's just me, it might go ok. We have a kind of truce, but you gotta trust me."

The painted words on the tree house wall came to her:

DON'T TRUST BISHOP

Did she really believe all the things Bishop said about her brother? For all she knew, that was Jesus on the motorcycle. He wouldn't need a Volvo after all, would he? The motorcycle's bellow grew louder. Bishop pushed her head farther into the seat, her cheek aching under Bishop's sweat-slicked palm.

"Oh shit," Bishop said.

"What?"

"He's crying."

Bishop's hand eased, and Jasmine lifted her head as the motorcycle passed. The rider wore a tattered kimono which fluttered in the wind. The cycle was crimson on chrome, all sharp arcs and low angles, a concept artist's imagination in living steel. It was something an astronaut would ride, not a filthy samurai with greasy, gnarled hair in a loose topknot.

Their eyes met. Red streams flowed from the samurai's eyes, branching across a grimy, tanned face. The rider seemed to recognize her, his eyes narrowed and he bared gleaming white teeth.

"Fuck all," Bishop said, and stomped his foot to the floor.

The motorcycle swerved around in an arc that should have sent it tumbling. The Blood Weeper leaned low to the ground, nearly horizontal, then cycle and rider came up gracefully in pursuit.

"Is this bad?"

"Are you particularly attached to your head?"

Jasmine swallowed. "Yes. Go faster."

"This is as fast as the Biscayne goes, babe."

"Then run him over or something."

"It's been tried. He's like a gazelle on that chopper. When the Blood Weeper starts crying, you run or you die."

"He doesn't look like any samurai I ever heard of."

Bishop gave her a lopsided grin. "This look like fuckin' Japan to you?"

The road ahead ran straight for miles. Jasmine was no race car driver, but she was sure the motorcycle would soon catch them. Bishop glanced in the rearview mirror.

"He's getting closer," she said.

"Yup, time to cheat."

Bishop felt around for his cassette case. He ran his finger down the row, stopping midway. He brought the cassette to his mouth, blew on the tape, and jammed it into the player. Then he started humming from the back of his throat.

The speakers erupted with four heavy bass drum beats followed by guitars chunking power chords. Jasmine clapped her hands to her ears and reached for the volume knob. Bishop slapped her hand.

"Sit back. Buckle up. No touch," he said and went back to humming. She reached for the seat belt and clicked it in.

He stuck a hand out the window, wiggling his fingers in time to the music. He banked his hand, and Jasmine felt a pressure in the air. Ahead in the heat shimmer, the straight road began to curve. She looked behind. The road seemed to stretch between them and the Blood Weeper, though the motorcycle continued to close.

Bishop checked the rearview mirror and grimaced. His fingers in the car's slipstream contorted into precise gestures. As the song launched into a guitar solo, his fingers flicked and formed shapes faster than her eyes could follow, becoming a blur as the solo worked to a fever pitch. Bishop's humming came in ragged breaths and the Biscayne drifted from the lane's center. As the guitar solo ended, Bishop's gesturing hand stopped and flew to the steering wheel. The road came to the top of a narrow canyon and curved along its lip. The meager gravel shoulder ended in a steep drop off to the canyon floor hundreds of feet below. Bishop twisted the steering wheel from side to side, following snake-like curves materializing from the heat shimmer.

"Come on, baby," he said.

The song changed abruptly and the Biscayne took the first turn a bit wide, the second wider. Bishop twisted the wheel over in short jerks, feet tapping the gas in a pattern Jasmine couldn't decipher. Tires squealed as the Biscayne fishtailed through more turns. Behind them, the Blood Weeper swept through the curves, holding his red cycle's balance like his tires were glued to the pavement. He matched them turn for turn, closing the gap. Twin blood streams painted his face red but for the whites of his eyes and shining teeth.

Out of the shimmer, a hairpin turn to the left appeared. The Biscayne slewed to the right. Bishop hummed a little riff, and a dirt berm rose from the gravel shoulder. There was no way Bishop could turn in time, she thought.

"Bishop—" she said.

"Hold the drift, you pig."

"Bishop—"

"And release," he said, cranking the wheel over.

The car's nose pulled left, too slow to make the turn. The bumper dipped as the front tires hit the gravel shoulder. Jasmine saw a red flash as the cycle passed behind. Bishop stomped his foot to the floor. The front end rose as it hit the berm, and they went airborne.

Jasmine's stomach clenched as they went over the edge. She had considered killing herself this way once, just taking a car at a hundred miles an hour into a tree or off a bridge. She had rejected the idea, afraid that somehow she would survive, paralyzed or comatose or something. Now, she wondered if it was because she hadn't wanted to die screaming.

Wish granted: she was too scared to scream.

The canyon passed beneath them, and a giant's hammer slammed her against the ceiling. Her head snapped back against something hard then whipped forward toward the dash. This was it, she thought. Please make it instantaneous. Then the giant's hand caught her by the chest and stopped her just short of oblivion. The Biscayne came to rest on the canyon's rim with a crunch. Bishop reached out and turned the radio off.

"Good girl," Bishop said.

"Thanks," Jasmine said. She looked over to see Bishop rubbing the dashboard.

"Good girl."

He opened the door and got out. Jasmine unbuckled and went out to join him. The car seemed different somehow. Its wheels were up into the fenders, and it had a weird twist to the body.

"Is it wrecked?" Jasmine said.

"She's not in good shape," Bishop said, "but she'll limp along."

The motorcycle's engine echoed through the canyon, growing closer.

"Do we run?" Jasmine said.

"Nah, we took out the ramp when we jumped. He doesn't have the angle to make it. "

The Blood Weeper brought his cycle to a stop on the other side. An angry voice shouted at them in Japanese.

"Do you understand what he's saying?" Bishop said.

"No," she said.

"Probably for the best. He's describing the order he's going to show you your organs before you die."

"What about you?"

"Nothing special. He's going to make me watch, then live-skin me before tossing me to some deaders."

He cupped his hands to his mouth. "You and what army, Kikuchiyo?"

Bishop grabbed his crotch in both hands and pumped his hips back and forth. The blood-covered samurai roared and unsheathed a sword. He leveled it at them and said something before starting his motorcycle and riding off.

"I don't think that helped," Jasmine said.

Bishop shrugged and walked back to the Biscayne.

"What did he say at the end?"

"That he's sworn to hunt us down, hang our heads from pointy sticks, blah, blah, blah."

"I don't think the crotch grab helped."

"He was going to kill us anyway once he saw you. Asshole's just being redundant."

"I guess your truce is off."

Bishop laughed. "That it is."

THE BISCAYNE SHUDDERED down the road, Bishop wincing with every knock, checking the rearview mirror every few seconds for dropped parts on the road. Jasmine figured they were doing about thirty miles an hour at the most, but it was hard to tell because the speedometer wasn't working. On this side of the canyon, the red rocks had given over to swells of green sandstone. The road cut through the petrified dunes like a shiny black ribbon. Occasionally, they would pass stands of trees, with naked branches bleached bone-white and bark peeling away like flayed skin.

"Where are we going?" Jasmine asked.

"We need to fix the car. The Blood Weeper will find a way around, and we can't outrun him like this."

"Can't you just do whatever you did back there again?"

"Limping along like this? Not a chance."

"What was that, anyway?"

"Just a thing. Badlands blessed, they call it."

"Can everyone here do it?"

"It's different for each person."

"Must be pretty useful."

Bishop frowned. "There's a saying. 'Badlands born, Badlands blessed, Badlands cursed.' However useful the blessing, there's a downside that tends to balance it out."

"So what's your curse?"

"Nothing you need to know about."

"Is that why Ryan didn't trust you?" It burst from her mouth before she could think about it.

Bishop stayed silent for a while. Jasmine wondered if he was thinking of kicking her out.

"How do you know your brother didn't trust me?"

"When I woke up here, there were some things written on the wall in his handwriting. He had written *Trust Bishop*, but it was painted over."

"Sounds about right," Bishop said. "He say anything else?"

"*Beware the Blood Weeper.*"

Bishop snorted. "Thank you, Captain Obvious."

"It also said *Follow the Lights to Paradise.*"

"Hmm."

"What?"

"Nothing."

"Why don't you tell me anyway," she said.

"Why don't you go wash the blood off my hood first?"

Jasmine inadvertently glanced at the bloodstains on the hood and swallowed. Her stomach turned, but she resolved not to show any more weakness in front of Bishop. Though it would serve him right if she puked in his precious car. They passed the day in silence, Bishop seemingly content with just driving, though Jasmine caught him staring at her legs several times. The man just smiled when she glared.

That evening, Bishop pulled the car off the road into a cleft running through a tall bluff.

"We'll hole up here for the night," Bishop said.

"Then what?"

"Tomorrow we should make it to a place I know where we can fix the car."

"And what after that? We just run around in circles out here until the Blood Weeper gets us?"

"I'm working on it."

No plan, then. Just like Ryan's burn-out friends from the real world. "Help me find Ryan," she said.

"No."

Jasmine saw her frown distorted back at her in Bishop's sunglasses. She wanted to go over there and rip them off.

"What does it mean to follow the lights to paradise?" she asked.

"It means getting your damn self killed."

"Big deal. I'm already dead."

"Says who?" He smirked at her, folding his arms and leaning back against the Biscayne.

"Says me."

"Right. So if you're dead already, why were you afraid of the deader last night?"

"That's different."

"Uh-huh. What if this paradise place ain't worth going to anyway?"

Jasmine paused, reminding herself that of course a guy who chose to stay in this hell would say anything to justify himself. "If that's where he is, that's where I'm going."

"He'll screw you over," Bishop said.

"How do you know?"

"Same as I know the sun will come up tomorrow and shit rolls downhill."

"I'm going to find him."

"Go right ahead. See you around." He smiled wider and waved.

"You're not helping?"

"Nope."

"But you have to, how am I supposed to find him by myself?"

Bishop shrugged and kicked a heel at the Biscayne's tire. "Dunno, but at least I'll still be alive. I'm all done with helping your brother out."

"But I need your help."

"I am helping, you just don't appreciate it yet, little girl."

Jasmine threw her hands in the air and walked away. The only car filled with food in a hell filled with zombies and blood-crying samurai, and it's driven by an impossible, dirty, smart-ass. She walked to the highway and kicked a rock down the centerline. When she left the bluff's shadow, the sun started baking her skin. The asphalt's heat seeped into her shoes.

She wouldn't last a day on her own. She knew that, of course. She'd have to go back to Bishop and figure out something, but she would be damned if she would apologize to him. She'd just have to convince him to help her some other way.

A nagging voice in the back of her head piped up. Yeah, how's that going to work? The only thing you have that's interested him so far is your body. How long will he wait until he just takes you?

I'll get a knife.

He'll just take it away from you. You'll screw it up somehow.

No way.

You always find a way.

The sun hovered just above the horizon, reminding her there were worse things roaming around than Bishop. She would have to be smart, tough, and wary. She would get her chance to find Ryan, but she needed help, even if it was in the form of Bishop. The first step was to stop this notion in his head that she was a little girl.

She turned around and walked back. Bishop appeared to be sleeping on the Biscayne's hood, but she suspected his eyes were open under his sunglasses. Was there a smirk at the corner of his mouth? Whatever. Let him smile as long as he kept his mouth shut.

Later, Bishop built a small fire and heated a can over the flames.

"What's for dinner?" Jasmine asked.

"Lima beans."

"Ew. Isn't there something else?"

"Probably, but tonight, we're having the beans."

"Why?"

"Because then tomorrow night's dinner will be all that much better."

"Blech. I hate beans. Got any water?"

"No," he said, "just drink what's at the bottom of the can."

Jasmine wrinkled her nose at the milky fluid bubbling around the pale beans and slimy casings, smelling of salt and metal.

"No way. You have it. I'll have water or something else."

"This ain't no restaurant, babe. You got to take what you can get."

He strummed off a guitar chord.

"Besides, it's good for you," he said.

"No."

She reached over Bishop for the canteen. He snatched it from her and held it out of reach. She looked up at him and she felt his stare from behind his sunglasses. His lips twitched as if he were fighting a smile.

"Fine," she said, "Have it your way."

Bishop let out a breath and shook his head.

"Not much fight in you is there?"

She went to the fire and stared at the can. She wanted to go home. She wanted a bath. She wanted a glass of wine, and then a pillow-topped bed. She wished she hadn't killed herself in the first place, though maybe she was in a coma, she didn't know. If all this was a coma, did that mean her subconscious hated her?

She kicked the can, scattering half its contents across the dirt. Bishop's guitar stopped.

"That was really dumb," he said.

He put down the guitar and went to her.

"Two things: if you're going to make it here, babe, you'll have to learn how to fight for what you want. Nobody's going to give you anything out here."

"You're helping me," she said.

"Yeah, but I'm different. There is only one Bishop in a whole world of ugly."

"So give me the water."

"No."

Jasmine dug her nails into her hands.

"Should I shoot you for it?"

"You don't even know how, yet. Which brings me to point two," Bishop said.

"Which is?"

"Survive. Everyone out here has learned to survive somehow. Some fight, some steal, some are clever, some are too batshit crazy to risk crossing. You need to find something that works, or you go deader in this place."

He knelt down before her and took off his sunglasses. His eyes were red-rimmed with dark circles under them. "Surviving is all there is. Got it?"

Jasmine wanted to look away, but his gaze held her. She eventually nodded.

"Good," he said. "Speaking of surviving—"

She tensed as he took a step toward her. Why hadn't she found a knife? But he stopped at the overturned can and brought it back to the fire. He produced a spoon and took a bite.

"Mmm. Warm and nutritious."

"Ryan always said they weren't beans but dried cockroach guts scraped from forklift tires at the bean factory."

Bishop smiled, white bits still stuck to his teeth.

Jasmine's stomach turned, and she looked away.

"Sorry," he said. "Look, I can put pepper on it, but you're going to have to eat some. We can't have you getting scurvy or whatever you get from not eating your beans."

She didn't say anything.

"I know you're hungry."

"I haven't been here long enough to get scurvy."

"Come on, baby," he leaned in closer, "for me?" He lifted his eyebrows and smirked.

She smiled despite herself and relaxed. He put on a hangdog look and held out the can to her.

"Fine. Give it here."

She choked down the chalky beans, trying not to think of cockroach innards. She even drank the bean juice.

4

She woke up with Bishop's arm draped over her. She screamed and kicked away from him, her legs tangling in the blanket. Bishop startled awake, one hand going to the pistol on the ground, the other fending off the blanket in his face.

"Bastard!"

"Hey, take it easy, babe. You were shivering last night."

"I'll bet."

"Nothing happened other than you getting a decent night's sleep, but go ahead and believe what you want."

How long had it been since Bishop had been with a woman? Too long, probably.

"Get this through your head, Bishop. Even if it snows, I sleep alone."

"Yeah, whatever," Bishop stood and gathered up the blanket. "If you want us freezing our asses off at night, then fine. Your virginity will never be in doubt."

"I'm not a vir—"

Bishop cocked an eyebrow.

"Yes?"

"Forget it."

She checked her clothes. All the buttons were fastened, with bra and underwear still in place. Her hips ached from sleeping on the hard ground, but not in a way as if she had had sex the night before. Goosebumps covered her arms and legs. She snatched the blanket from Bishop's hands and wrapped it around her.

"Can we just find my brother? Can we follow the lights to paradise or whatever?"

"Paradise City doesn't exist," Bishop said. "Your brother is delusional."

"So it's a myth? Why would he lie me?"

"He was obsessed with the idea. He wanted everything to be perfect, one place where he could live forever. Then one day just up and leaves to go find it."

"And did he?"

"Said he did, told us all to come along, leave the broken things behind, and start fresh. Told us to follow the lights to paradise."

Bishop spat.

"Why didn't you go with him?"

"Someone had to stay behind, didn't they? Round up all the stragglers hiding from the deaders and the Blood Weeper? Your brother couldn't be bothered. He had to go play God in the new paradise, so I stayed behind."

"But there's no one left. You could go there now, couldn't you?"

Bishop began gathering up his things.

"Well, can't you?"

"You know, a few months, maybe a year after he left, I found out paradise wasn't so fucking hot.

"One day, I'm near the edge of the Badlands, at this bridge that crosses over to your brother's promised land. I see this blimp coming in the haze—an airship I think they call it. It flies over and lands. These guys with guns get out. Then this tight little circle of refugees is pushed out. One of them breaks loose, shouts something, and starts running back to the ship. A moment later, he's clubbed over the head.

"I reach them as the airship is taking off and recognize the guy with his head caved in. I had helped him escape to Paradise City the month before. Two or three more in the crowd are people I've helped too. I mean these are people I bled for, you know?

"I shout up to the airship, 'what the fuck,' right? These guys fought hard to get to Paradise City. There's nothing for them here, they went to see their God in the promised land. Hell, their God promised them the promised land. Then this guy sticks his head out the window, looks down at me, and he smiles. Do you know what he said to me?"

"No."

"Paradise is full."

"Ryan wouldn't do that," Jasmine said.

Bishop shrugged.

"Your brother isn't the same guy I first met."

"What happened to the others?"

"Most went back across the bridge, following the airship. Maybe they wouldn't make it all the way back to Paradise City, but they would find something else, they said. Probably croaked by now, fighting deaders, the Weeper, or each other."

"Couldn't you help them?"

"Maybe one or two, yeah. But fifty? I pointed out the nearest food dump, gave them a spare gun or two, and wished them well. I never saw them again."

"Then why are you helping me?"

"I wonder the same thing. Maybe it's been so long since I saw anyone, I couldn't help myself."

"Are you going to help me find Ryan?"

Bishop shook his head."I'm going to find you somewhere safe. Right now that's not Paradise City or anywhere near your brother."

ON THE HIGHWAY, Bishop turned on the radio but there was only Eighties music. After twenty minutes of non-stop odes to sex, money, and parties, Jasmine made him turn it off. They rode in silence for two hours and Jasmine didn't know how Bishop could stand it: the howling wind whipping through the open windows, the way the yellow centerline dashes blended together, or how the car's broken engine let out a sour odor that made it seem like they were being pickled in some bizarre way. The red-gashed hills had grown larger, a few morphed into flat-topped mesas, and Jasmine half expected Indians on horseback looking down on them like from some movie.

She looked at Bishop. He was no John Wayne. The Duke would have kicked Bishop's ass and given him a haircut. Her musing was cut short when Bishop turned off the highway onto a dirt road. Yellowed pines lined the road, providing a macabre shade for the dead grass underneath. After the endless parade of red hills and mesas, she found the change of scenery almost pleasant.

"So what now?" she asked.

"Supplies," he said.

He reached out and flicked out his middle finger at the gas gauge, which Jasmine had to lean over to see. The needle was close to resting on "E." When she looked up, she thought she saw Bishop's eyes flick back to the road. Had he been looking down her shirt? She couldn't be sure. She sat back and sidled closer to the door.

"Why aren't there gas stations closer to the road?"

Bishop just looked at her in a way that made her feel like a child.

"No gas stations, I take it," she said.

"No, there are gas stations, just no gas at the pumps. Or if there is, it's guarded by crazy nuts with towers and barricades or overrun by deaders just waiting for some meat desperate enough to try and come get it. Your brother never made as many gas stations as he did grocery stores. We partied at lot more back then and didn't move around as much."

"So are we going to sneak into a nut-job's gas station?"

He shook his head. "Nope, we're going someplace safe where we can fix the Biscayne."

"And then what?"

"Then I figure out what to do with you."

THEY CAME to a slight rise in the road blocked by a rusty gate. Bishop opened the door and walked up to it. Jasmine followed, grateful for the opportunity to stretch her legs. The gate had once been white before it had turned to rust, and to either side a ten-foot-high fence topped with razor wire coils ran into the forest. A chain with links as big around as Jasmine's finger wrapped around the bars, secured with a gleaming silver padlock. Jasmine lifted the lock.

"Why isn't it rusty like everything else?"

"Stainless steel. Won't rust," Bishop said.

"So how do we get in?"

"We announce ourselves."

Bishop knelt by the gate and reached though the bars. He picked up what looked like a metal egg or a tea infuser from the dirt and pulled. As he pulled the wire back, dirt flew into the air as a pulley and rope jerked from the packed ground. Bishop grunted and pulled the rope through the bars.

Bishop pulled a folded piece of paper and a pencil nub from his back pocket. He wrote something on the paper and put it in the tea infuser. He motioned Jasmine to come closer.

"Pull this rope while I hold the pulley."

Jasmine grasped the dirty nylon rope and pulled. As she worked, the infuser and its note jerked its way down the road. Hand over hand, she pulled the rope and watched the note disappear over the rise like laundry being run out on the line. A few minutes later, the rope ground to a halt and she couldn't make it budge any farther.

"It's stuck," she said.

"Just wait," Bishop said and sat down on the ground, leaning his head against the gate. "If it starts moving, make sure the pulley doesn't slip through the gate's bars."

"Huh?"

"It'll be a while. In the meantime, let me rest for a second, okay?"

Jasmine realized he had been driving all day. "Uh, okay, sure."

Bishop readjusted his sunglasses, and soon his head slumped to the side. His breathing slowed and he was out within a minute.

Jasmine wiped the sweat off her forehead and rubbed at the rope burns on her hands. She looked up and watched the clouds. They were the same little wisps and commas she remembered from the day before. The winds seemed to push them along at a good pace, and she wished a breeze could come down here and cool the place down a bit. Her polo was plastered to her back. The clouds didn't care. They just floated along as the wind took them. They seemed to curl a bit counter-clockwise, like they were being pulled into a giant drain far, far away.

Off in the distance, several crows cawed. Were they alive or deaders, she wondered. The rope jerked once, twice, and Jasmine had just enough time to grab at the pulley as it skittered toward the gate.

"Bishop!" she said. He awoke in an instant and reached around her to help hold the pulley. He was hot and sweaty and had the smell of someone who hadn't bathed in weeks. She shoved an elbow back against his stomach, which didn't seem to do much. It was like hitting a tree. He grunted and pulled her in tighter.

She wanted to drop the pulley, but his hands were clamped over hers. She bucked back against him, trying to break free.

"Hold it, dammit," he said, "don't you dare let this go." His grip tightened like a vice.

"Let me go," she said.

The thoughts came in a flash. Long days on the road by himself, frustrated that she didn't just blow him on the spot for saving her life, using this excuse to make his move. She was going to end up in the trunk, tied up with her own underwear.

She stomped on his shin, dragging it down to the instep like her old Hawaiian-Okinawan sensei had taught her. Had she done it properly, it would have broken his shin. Instead, she just pissed Bishop off.

Lights flashed in her eyes and pain bloomed purple behind her left ear. She went down to the ground. She rolled up and ran to the car. She reached in and pulled the machete free as she spun around.

Bishop was down to one knee with his arm stretched all the way through the gate. He grimaced and grunted as he pulled back. The tea egg dangled from the rope wrapped around Bishop's swelling, purple fingers.

"What the fuck?" he yelled. He rattled the metal egg. "What did I tell you to do?"

She held the machete between them. "Don't come any closer."

"Or else what, little girl? You gonna stick me with that?" He took a limping step. "You gonna live out here in deader central with fresh blood on the ground and a car with an empty tank?"

Her mind flashed the image of blood-frenzied zombies surrounding her, pounding on the car's windows to get at her.

"I don't know, but you're not going to lay another hand on me."

"We can discuss your delicate sensibilities later, little girl. For now," he tossed the tea egg at her feet. "Put that pig sticker away and open this." He held up his left hand. A red crease stretched across his palm, pink on one side, purple on the other. "Thanks to you, I can't feel a damn thing in my hand."

You screwed up, said a voice in the back of her head. *You knew you would.*

"You hit me, Bishop, I didn't think—"

"After you tried breaking my leg," he said. "Start realizing I'm your only friend in the Badlands or start learning how to fight off deaders on your own." He limped forward and pushed past the machete to get into the front seat. Jasmine reached down and grabbed the egg from the dirt. She unscrewed the top and dumped a key into her hand. Her eyes stung, but she wouldn't let Bishop see her wipe at them. She walked to the gate, letting the machete's heavy tip drag in the dirt.

Screwed it up again, Jas. If you're lucky, he'll slit your throat in your sleep before he leaves you to those deader things. He could have done anything to you at any time, and you freak out like some prissy bitch. You're such a child.

The key turned easily in the lock. She unraveled the chains and opened the gate, looking away as Bishop drove past.

"Lock up behind me," he said.

She closed the gate, afraid Bishop would leave her there, but the car stopped and idled while she replaced the chains and refastened the lock. She walked slowly back to the passenger side.

The machete landed on the blankets in the backseat. Bishop drove with his right hand on the wheel while his left sat in his lap like a dead thing. She turned away and rubbed at her eyes with the back of her hand.

As they topped the rise, Jasmine gasped. The road crossed concentric ditches like a scene from World War I. Bishop eased the car over a creaking plank bridge spanning the first gap. She looked down and saw the pits were filled with sharpened stakes; a few still impaled desiccated bodies: bodies face down, bodies face up, bodies missing limbs, and bodies whittled down to mere lumps. Black birds hopped from stake to stake, tilting their heads at each body before deciding whether to take a sample or move on.

Between the ditches were rolls and rolls of rusted razor wire. Tattered pieces of clothing, skin, and hair fluttered from the barbs in the light breeze. One crow played tug of war with the wire over a stringy mass. Another crow landed and the two started to fight, squawking and pecking at each other.

"So many bodies," she said.

"They form living bridges. One goes down, and the others step over it to get to the next ditch."

"How can anyone survive here?"

"Foo."

"What's foo?"

"You'll see."

Five groaning bridges and body-lined pits later, they topped another rise. Three more trenches surrounded a decaying wooden house nestled in a yard filled with scrap metal. The weathered gray siding had bits of white paint stubbornly holding in spots; the roof was a patchwork of black tar paper and individual green shingles like islands on a dark sea. Beyond the tangle of metal tubing, burned-out car bodies, wheelbarrows without tires, paint cans, old bike frames, twisted swing sets, a green fiberglass boat, and other bits and pieces of bric-a-brac, she saw boarded windows. The whole area smelled like gasoline and diesel, rich noxious petrochemical vapors that had up until this point reminded Jasmine of mowing the lawn.

On the upper story over the rotting front porch, words had been spray-painted in red: LOVE SHACK.

As Bishop navigated the last bridges, Jasmine found the inner trenches spike-free. Instead, a metal pipe ran the length of each with spigots spaced every five or six feet. There were no bodies here, just the odd blackened rock or two; or so she thought until she realized one of the rocks had a shoulder and elbow attached.

"They've been burned," she said. It sounded stupid as soon as it came out. Jasmine Shaw, master of the obvious.

"Foo gas," Bishop said as he leaned his head out the window, looking down at the tires. He moved the steering wheel gingerly. "Gasoline and soap, sort of a homemade napalm."

"It stops them?"

"Hells yes it does. It's sticky, it flows, and it burns. Damn nasty. As the deaders rub up against each other, it transfers." The car rocked as they came off the bridge. "Pretty soon—poof! No more deader apocalypse."

"There must be a lot of them."

"Yup."

They parked at the junk pile's edge, "within the first foo ring" as Bishop called it. A barely noticeable footpath switched back on itself, in some cases requiring them to get on hands and knees to crawl through the twisted metal maze. They emerged on a front porch every bit as convoluted as the junk pile maze with rotten boards, gaping holes, and rusty nails. Jasmine wondered if there weren't rings, spigots, or barrels otherwise rigged to engulf them in flame if they stepped the wrong way.

Bishop carefully made his way to the front door, testing each step before he committed his weight. Jasmine followed him step-for step, catching up as he put his hand on the front door's handle.

"Wait," said Jasmine, "shouldn't you knock first?"

"What, with this?" He held up his crippled left hand. Jasmine felt her face flush. "If she didn't want us to come in, we would have been dead a long, long time ago."

She? Did Bishop have a girlfriend squirreled away in here?

He turned the doorknob with his right hand and entered. Jasmine followed, stepping around a rusted nail waiting to nick her ankle.

She couldn't believe the place could be worse on the inside. The love shack looked like a tenement that even squatters would abandon. The plaster walls were cracked and had fallen away, exposing rib-like slats. The mold on the walls and ceiling couldn't even settle on whether to color the place brown, yellow, or black. Bits of plaster, slat board, and wallpaper were embedded in the carpet that had once been red but was now a speckled pink. Somewhere, something rotten released a sulfur smell that cut through the gasoline fumes. Maybe the house itself was rotting and they were just touring the carcass, Jasmine thought.

"Lucy, I'm home!" Bishop said in a fair Ricky Ricardo.

"In here," a woman's voice called.

They stepped over a threadbare sofa cushion in brown-and-black plaid. Their host stood in front of the matching sofa, under a mirrored disco ball with her hands clasped expectantly before her.

"Bishop!" she said and ran to him. He caught her with his good hand as she jumped into an embrace. He spun her around, sending her yellow skirt twirling.

"Is he coming? Is he here?" she asked. She got on her tiptoes and looked past Bishop. When she saw Jasmine, her smile fell a little. There was something familiar about her, Jasmine thought.

She was about five two, blonde hair to the chin, with sapphire-blue eyes. She wore a yellow tulle party dress, all ruffles in the skirt, sash tied at the waist, bare at the shoulders and arms. She was the very image of a 50s prom queen and should have been pretty, but the effect was ruined. Her legs were covered by hose with several holes and runs threatening to sunder the garment entirely. Her skirt had a tear at the bottom and the ghost of an oil spot not quite washed out. Her makeup was streaky too, like she had been crying or had slept with makeup still on. Instead of the prom queen triumphant, she was the prom queen pathetic. But where, Jasmine wondered, had she met her before?

The girl's eyes went wide, and she suddenly beamed at Jasmine.

"Ohmygod, you look just like him!" she said. "Well not just like him, obviously but you know what I mean, right? You've both got the same gorgeous eyes. You're his sister, aren't you? I just knew it." She looked back over her shoulder at Bishop, who nodded.

"Yeah, this is Jasmine. I picked her up on the road."

The girl opened her arms and stepped in for an embrace. "Well welcome to the Love Shack, Jas. I'm Cally—that's like Kelly but with an 'a'—and I just know we're going to be the best of friends."

Jasmine punched her in the face. Cally's head snapped to the side, and she fell to the ground.

The name had clicked in her head and she remembered, oh she remembered all right. The hair, the eyes, the set of the face. How could she have ever forgotten?

"You bitch," Jasmine said.

She reached down and grabbed a fistful of blonde hair. She pulled Cally to her knees.

"What's the matter," Jasmine said, "ruining our lives once wasn't enough, you had to follow us into hell too?"

Anger filled her, seeping into all the hollow places in her body. She cocked her fist back. Bishop's hand seized Jasmine's arm before she could launch.

"What the fuck, Jasmine?" Bishop said.

"What the hell is she doing here, Bishop?" Jasmine asked.

She tried to shuck Bishop's grip on her arm, but his hand wouldn't budge. Her head lowered, and she glared at the woman whose eyes had just started to refocus.

"That blue-eyed bitch ruined everything for me."

"Bishop?" Cally said.

Jasmine tried kicking her, but Bishop pulled her back. Someone screamed, and Jasmine fell to the floor. Her hand came away with tufts of Cally's hair. Cally scrambled on her knees then got to her feet and ran into the next room.

"Jasmine, calm down," Bishop said.

Her anger went up a notch. Calm down? Who was he to tell her that? Then Bishop put himself between her and Cally's escape route.

Bishop said, "Cally isn't who you think she is; I guarantee it. Whoever you think she is, she isn't. You have to believe me. She's a friend."

Jasmine shook her head.

"You don't understand, Bishop, she's no friend. I don't care what she's said to you in the past. She's trouble."

"Cut it with the blitzkrieg and think."

"Like hell." Jasmine snarled.

She ran past Bishop's left side. His swollen fingers landed on her arm but couldn't close in time. She cleared the ratty couch and shot through the doorway. There was a blur to her left as she cleared the door jamb. Lights flashed in her eyes, and for the second time that day, she found herself down. Blood trickled in thin streams from her nose, and the world looked like it was smeared with Vaseline.

The great yellow blob she assumed as Cally held a smaller black blob in her hands. Cally reversed her grip and pointed the blob at Jasmine's head. Jasmine heard the shick-clack echo in the room as Cally racked in a shotgun shell. The cool barrel kissed her forehead.

"Stay down, Jasmine." Bishop's voice said from behind her. "Cally won't think twice about laying you out."

As the tears cleared from her vision, Cally came into focus. She saw the woman staring down at her with hard, clear eyes and a growing dark spot on her face where the punch had landed. Jasmine remembered the staked pits outside, the razor wire, the foo gas, and all the blackened bodies outside the front door.

"Really, honey," Cally said, "Let's just calm down."

Jasmine got up slowly and turned her back on Cally. She pinched her nose gingerly. It was swelling, probably broken. She wiped the blood with the back of her hand several times, noting the flow didn't seem to lessen.

Footsteps approached and held out something white. She took the gauze and pressed it gently against her nose.

"Thanks," she said.

"We done now?" Cally said.

"Yeah." You gotta sleep sometime, bitch. Then we'll see.

"Come on. Let's get some ice for her nose and my hand."

Ice? There's ice in hell?

"Oh Bishop," Cally said. The hard woman instantly turned into a cooing nursemaid, like she had discovered a baby bird fallen from its nest. "What happened?"

"Got it caught on the way here." He looked at Jasmine and gave a barely perceptible shake of his head. "No big deal, just some swelling."

"Well let's get that fixed," Cally said. "Jas, we'll set your nose once the swelling goes down. Until then, there are more bandages in the kit over there." She pointed to a white box sitting on the floor in the corner. "I'll go get some ice."

Bishop waited until Cally had walked down the hall.

"What's the problem?"

She waved him away. "Forget it."

He looked at her just like Dad had when she was six, waiting for a better answer.

"Wait until this is better, okay?" She waved her hand around her nose.

"Okay, but you gotta cut this crap out. People are trying to help you, Jasmine."

"Sorry."

What the hell was she supposed to say? That her brother was normal until Kelly Jaque showed up at their house all bleached hair and boobs? That from then on he was wherever she was, listening to her vapid diatribes on why bands where the lead singer played guitar were superior to those who didn't? He pretended not to care but snuck peeks at her when he thought she wasn't looking. What a dork. Jasmine couldn't tell what he saw in her. Because of her, he began worshipping at the altar of hair metal. Because of her, he grew out his hair and wore an acid-washed jean jacket. Because of her, he tried to fit in with the burners at school. And because of her, he snuck out on his seventeenth birthday while Jasmine slept, went to a party, and never came back.

Kelly never knew, of course, that Ryan had a thing for her. Someone must have blabbed about it after the accident because she showed up at the viewing looking like a martyr. She brought a single white rose and laid it in the coffin with him. When she sat back down, she burst into tears and was immediately swarmed by a gaggle of her fellow burner skanks. It made Jasmine sick. Like Kelly knew anything about Ryan, or had even a right to feel sorry for herself over him. Kelly couldn't begin to fathom the idiocy she inspired in Jasmine's brother.

Kelly tried coming around once after the funeral. She knocked on the door and stared at her feet while Jasmine walked to open the door. Her hand stopped short of the doorknob. It shook, and Jasmine couldn't stop it. Kelly wasn't satisfied ruining just one life, now she was back to start ruining another. As Jasmine looked through the front door's window, Kelly looked up and their eyes met. The other girl's eyes were red and puffy and mascara bled down her face. Kelly shifted from foot to foot, tried to put on a small smile.

Jasmine forced her face to remain smooth; she let herself go numb. She leveled a cold stare at Kelly and thought the words as loud as she could at the girl on the other side of the glass. *You are the cause of all this. You are nothing to me now. Go away.*

Perhaps her crude attempt at telepathy worked. Maybe it was just the words fueling the look in her eyes. Or maybe it was just the fact that after a few moments, Jasmine turned around and walked away, leaving Kelly to stare at her back, all alone on the porch. At any rate, Jasmine never saw Kelly again.

5

Cally walked into the room with two ice bags. Jasmine saw that while the resemblance was uncanny, there were differences in the woman. Kelly was pretty in only the most common way, getting attention for her blue eyes and a chest that made up for lack of quality with gross quantity. Jasmine always thought Kelly looked squished—fat really—like five-foot-ten worth of body on a five-foot-four frame. Cally was different: her hair fairer, eyes whiter, hips narrower, breasts higher, cheekbones more defined. Cally walked with a straight back where Kelly had a stoop to her shoulders like she was afraid all the time. Oddly, Cally was shorter than her real-world counterpart. Cally was all of five-two, just the right size, Jasmine supposed, so her head would fit under Ryan's chin.

"Here you go, Jas," Cally said, handing her an old plastic grocery bag. Cally shared Kelly's same Texas twang. Jasmine set the ice bag on her face and let the cold numb the pain.

"So how's it been, Cally?" Bishop asked. His left hand had been bandaged and wrapped with ice.

She leaned back on the couch and stared at the disco ball. "About the same. Deaders attack every few weeks, I clear the pits and make more foo."

"Why do they keep attacking?" Jasmine asked.

Cally dangled a yellow pump from her foot. "Don't know. Maybe they used to come here and party when they were alive. The music, the lights, the dancing," she looked at Jasmine and winked. "The sex wasn't bad either." She gave a little squeal that led into a sigh. "I think they somehow remember all the good times and come back for more."

"And get impaled, eviscerated, or immolated," Bishop said.

Cally laughed. "It's not like they're coming to dance and fuck." Bishop snorted and Jasmine glared at him.

"It's horrible," Jasmine said. "You know who these people were?"

Cally shrugged and rolled to her back. "Whattya gonna do? I gotta keep this place open in case he comes back."

"Who?"

Cally looked back at her, upside-down. "Him." When Jasmine didn't say anything, Cally rolled her eyes. "Your brother." She looked back at the disco ball and sighed. "I remember when I first saw him, so shy at first, but I got him to come out of his shell. After that, we were inseparable."

I bet, Jasmine thought.

"We would dance and dance, laugh, sing, get drunk, and go to bed. In the morning, we'd wake up and do it all over again." Cally glanced back at Jasmine. "Does that bother you, honey?"

"You going to break my nose again if it does?"

Cally laughed. "He was happy with me, Jas. He was so uptight when I first met him, so scared about everything. He said with me, it was the first time he felt like he was alive."

"I'm sure," Jasmine said and smiled sweetly. "So why'd he leave you?"

Cally's smile disappeared as she turned away. *Score one for me*, Jasmine thought.

"That's enough, Jasmine," Bishop said.

"Hey, I'm just trying to figure things out here, remember?"

Bishop pointed at her nose. "Yeah, and you're doing it the hard way. Lay off her for a bit, okay?"

Jasmine bit off a retort as Bishop walked over to Cally and laid a hand on her arm.

"We need gas and a place to hole up while I fix my car. I've got some extra food, plus detergent for your foo."

Cally stood and walked to a boarded up window with her hands wrapped tightly around herself. She squinted through a small hole as she spoke. "Pull your Chevy around back."

"One other thing, we ran into the Blood Weeper out there. He's after us too."

"Like I care. The Blood Weeper can kiss my ass."

"Thanks, Cally," Bishop said. "I appreciate it."

⁓

BISHOP'S FEET stuck out from under the Biscayne. Jasmine sat on an upside-down plastic bucket next to the car, feeling like a bug caught in a spider's web. Steel cables and nylon ropes crisscrossed the area, suspending steel I-beams, junked out car chassis, refrigerators, and bed springs. It had taken most of a day to get the Biscayne maneuvered through the convoluted path. For a week, Bishop pulled the frame straight and hammered out the worst dents. Jasmine watched and helped where she could, and stayed in the shade when she could not. The alternative was spending time with Cally, which was hard enough when work stopped at sundown and the three of them were cooped up in the house together. Cally talked incessantly about herself and insinuated she and Jasmine were sisters. Bishop grew grumpier each day, though Jasmine couldn't tell why. Still, she rather liked working with Bishop because he was quiet. He murmured to himself, mostly, unless he needed something.

"Wrench, nine-sixteenths," he said.

As Jasmine went for the wrench, the wind picked up and she flinched as wooden frames groaned and a refrigerator's shadow swayed over her. Jasmine kept one eye overhead and picked the wrench from a pile of rust-spotted tools at her feet. The gravel dug into her knees as she got down and handed it to Bishop. He grunted, as near a thank-you as she had gotten since they started work that morning.

"Dammit, Jas, I said nine-sixteenths, not seven."

The wrench rang as it skipped across the gravel.

"It looked like a nine to me," Jasmine said.

She rummaged through the tool pile until she found the nine-sixteenths.

"Here," she said.

Bishop grunted.

Jasmine turned as footsteps approached. Cally appeared from behind a tower of dishwashers.

"How's it going, guys?"

"Oh just marvelous," Jasmine said. "When he's not cursing under there, he disappears around the junk piles for up to an hour, looking for parts."

Bishop slid out and sat up. Black grease, dust, and sweat coated his chest and arms. Blood glistened on gouged knuckles.

"The major work is done, but I've still got some things to button up."

"You going to finally fix the speedometer on that thing?"

Bishop shrugged.

"Not unless you have more parts around here I don't know about."

Cally gave him a wicked smile. "I have plenty of parts you don't know about. Would you like to see?"

Bishop shifted uncomfortably.

"Oh don't be that way," Cally said.

To Jasmine, she said, "He's always been so shy. Cute, isn't it?"

Bishop, shy?

"I'm just not going to mess with someone else's old lady," Bishop said.

"We don't have to tell him," Cally said in a stage whisper. She winked at Jasmine.

"Not today, Cally," Bishop said.

"Fine, have it your way. Say, do you happen to have any cigarettes?"

Bishop smiled and reached for a blue flannel shirt hanging on the Biscayne's side-view mirror. He reached inside the pocket and tossed a cigarette to Cally.

"It's my last one."

"Liar," Cally said.

She caught the lighter Bishop tossed and lit her cigarette.

"That's not good for you," Jasmine said.

Cally held the cigarette between her index and middle finger as she rounded her lips and exhaled.

"They'll kill you," Jasmine said.

"Maybe," Cally said, "But when I become a deader, you'll be able to hear me wheeze. I'm doing you a favor."

She tossed the lighter back to Bishop, and pointed at the Biscayne with her cigarette.

"You know, Bishop, there's enough scrap metal around here for you to turn that into a tank."

"That's all right, Cally, I'd rather just keep it as it is."

Cally shrugged.

"Thanks for the ciggie. I'm off to check the foo barrels for leaks."

Cally walked off, puffing on the cigarette and humming a tune. Jasmine stared at Cally's back, wondering how the woman stayed so chipper in this little pocket of hell.

"Relax, babe, she's joking," Bishop said.

"About becoming an emphysemic deader or smoking around napalm?" He smiled.

"Still," Jasmine said, looking over her shoulder to make sure Cally was out of earshot, "she has a point. Why don't you armor this thing?"

Bishop leaned back against the car and rolled his head toward her.

"You put armor on stuff you expect to get hit. I don't work that way."

"What? You don't expect to get in a fight?"

"Not if I can help it. Running away has worked out pretty well so far."

"What about the Blood Weeper?'

"Armor wouldn't have helped against him. In fact, it would have been harder bending the road with extra weight."

"So no armor."

"All my tricks are set up for this car going a certain speed and holding a line through the turns. Even having your skinny ass in the car makes a difference. With an extra ton of scrap metal hanging off? Forget it."

"And the speedometer's broken."

"Yup, but between the rhythm of the centerline dashes and the music, we get by."

"What if you have to go off the highway?"

"Well, let's just hope it doesn't come to that."

JASMINE SAT in the Biscayne's driver's seat, tapping a fingertip against the steering wheel. Cally sat next to her, filing a nail.

"Try it," Bishop called out.

Jasmine turned the key, and the Biscayne's engine whinnied as it tried to start.

"Ho—Stop!" Bishop said. A ratchet began clicking. Jasmine sighed and slumped back against the seat. Two hours sitting in the heat with nothing to do but stare at the car's hood through the windshield or make small talk with Cally. The conversation ran dry in the first ten minutes.

"This sucks," Jasmine said.

"You gotta have patience. Or you gotta make your own fun."

"Yeah? What's there to do around here that's fun?"

Cally got a malicious glint in her eye and leaned out of the open door.

"Bishop, you want to help me wash my hair?"

"That's all right, I gotta get this working right now," Bishop said, not looking up from the engine. "Besides, you know what your old man would say if he found out?"

"I'm sure he'd understand."

The ratcheting stopped. "I really gotta get this done, Cally."

"Fine," Cally said. She turned to Jasmine and shrugged. "Well, I tried."

"He's worried about the car," Jasmine said. "He's been so busy with it since we got here."

"Honey, he's always busy. I used to think he just wasn't into blondes. Then along came Jenna, she was Swedish. Then maybe I thought my boobs were too big, but he hooked up with that top-heavy Tina—how she managed to balance on those tiny feet I don't know."

"You're coming on to him pretty strong. I never gave him a hint and was all but dropping his pants every five minutes. Maybe you should turn it down a notch."

"Honey, Bishop ain't into subtle. With a man, you gotta give him the signals loud and clear even if they do walk around with their pants around their ankles half the time. Back in the day, the girl that got together with Bishop was the one who could make him notice her over the skanks that dropped their panties after the first beer.

"For all intents, Bishop and I are the closest thing to the last man and woman in the Badlands, and he wouldn't touch me even if I were strutting naked right in front of him. I know because I tried it once. Can you believe that bastard looked away and blushed? Him?" Cally shook her head. "That boy ain't right."

"I thought you were waiting for Ryan to come back."

Cally smiled and covered her mouth with one hand.

"Yeah," she said, "but until he does, a girl's got to have her fun, right?"

Jasmine smiled back in spite of herself. "I guess so."

"Tell you what, you can have Bishop. I'm through with him."

"I don't really—"

"Oh shush. Not right now, but sometime you're going to want a little. Bishop's a bit skinny but he should be able to scratch the itch."

"Right," Jasmine said, shifting in her seat.

"Give it another try," Bishop said.

The engine whinnied and coughed but wouldn't turn over.

"Hold up," Bishop said.

"Think about it," Cally said. She slid from the car and walked to the house.

~

JASMINE DREAMED OF APPLES. Her teeth pierced the skin and plunged deeply. The sweet crispy flesh tasted like a summer day. The crunch filled her ears, and she enjoyed the efficiency of her jaw as it turned the flesh to pulp. As she swallowed, she turned the apple until pristine skin faced her. She bit again, larger this time so that she had to rip the flesh free. It was again glorious, though not so much as the first bite. The first bite was always the sweetest. She wiped away the juice dripping down her chin with the back of her hand, cool and sticky. She hadn't had an apple in years, why was that? How could she have forgotten how damn good an apple was?

Jasmine woke up to power chords. She looked up at Bishop standing at her feet, guitar in hand. His right arm windmilled in time to his words.

"Wake … up … Jasmine."

He paused with his arm in the air and looked at her.

"Get bent," she said.

Bishop grinned and brought his arm down, strumming jackhammer-quick.

"Time to wake up … time to wake up … yeah."

The sound hit her between the eyes. She put both hands over her ears and turned over, but the audio assault continued.

"Time to up and shit and shave … you can sleep more when you're in the grave …"

"Shut up," Jasmine yelled.

"Time to get up and jam … Cally's fryin' up some Spam, oh yeahhhhh…"

Jasmine threw a couch cushion at Bishop. He swayed out of its way.

"I can see that you're good and pissed … Else you would not have missed …" he sang.

She sat up. "I'm gonna ram that thing right down your throat."

"Said the farmer to the goat—"

Jasmine leapt off the couch and lunged at Bishop. Bishop ran, keeping the couch between them.

"Fine, asshole, I'm up," she said.

"And a fine good morning to you too, baby," Bishop said.

"I'm not your baby."

"If you say so."

Jasmine pulled back and swung her palm at his face. Bishop moved rattlesnake-quick and lightly slapped her wrist away. Jasmine led with her other hand, but he blocked it before she could connect.

"Fuck!" she said and walked away.

"Oh come on, Jas," Bishop said after her.

She turned. "What?"

Bishop's lips wriggled.

"Don't you want to hear my encore?"

His grin burst out, larger than ever.

Jasmine left the room, and wove her way around the boxes and debris in the hallway toward the back door leading to the outhouse. It seemed like everyone here knew how to fight. You shouldn't need to know how to fight in heaven. It wasn't fair. None of this was fair.

After breakfast, Jasmine tapped Cally on the shoulder.

"Teach me how to shoot," she said.

"Really? I thought you didn't like guns."

"I hate them. There's no need for them back home, but out here? I think I need to know how to use one."

"Why not ask Bishop?"

"Because I think he'd use it as an excuse to cop a feel."

"What makes you think I won't?" Cally winked.

Jasmine stared at her. She opened her mouth a few times, wondering how to respond when Cally burst out laughing.

"Honey, I'm kidding. Oh your face! Priceless."

Cally grabbed her by the hand.

"Don't worry, honey, your chastity is safe with me. Now let's go learn how to defend it."

CALLY HELD what looked like a rusted metal sculpture attached to a wooden rifle stock.

"What's this?" Jasmine asked.

"It's a crossbow," Cally said.

"I want to know how to shoot a gun, not become some medieval reenactor."

"You gotta walk before you can fly, hon. Besides, we can't spare the ammunition right now for anything more modern."

"Okay." Jasmine couldn't keep the uncertainty from her voice.

"Don't worry, once you get the hang of this, I'll show you how to handle a shotgun."

Cally pointed to the crossbow. "This is the string, it shoots the bolt."

"I thought it shot arrows."

Cally held up a metal rod just a bit longer than her hand. It had sharp triangular barbs at the head and thin plastic feathers at the tail.

"We don't have arrows, we have bolts. Get over it."

"Okay."

Cally put the crossbow's nose to the ground and put her foot in a metal loop jutting out from the weapon's front. She then pulled the string back with a grunt.

"You put your foot in the stirrup here to keep this mother steady while you load. When the latch clicks, you can put the bolt in."

She put the bolt into a groove running along the top and slid it back until it met the string.

"There's a spring here on top to keep the bolt in place until you're ready to fire. Just don't expect it to hold if you start doing jumping jacks with it, okay?"

Jasmine rolled her eyes. "No calisthenics with the weapon. Got it."

"Shut up and listen," Cally said. Jasmine opened her mouth to argue but thought better of it as Cally glared. Cally pointed to two dots near the trigger.

"This is the safety. If the button is under the white dot, it's not supposed to fire." Cally looked up. "Don't trust it. Shit breaks sometimes. Don't point a loaded *anything* at anyone even if the safety is on, got it?"

Jasmine nodded.

"Okay, you put your hands here and here, pull the butt tight into your shoulder, and look down the groove. This thing doesn't have sights, so you'll have to estimate the range and how much the bolt's gonna drop."

"How do I do that?"

Cally smiled.

"Practice. When you're ready to fire, take the safety off—that's the red dot —line up your shot, and shoot."

Cally pointed the crossbow at a blue plastic barrel and pulled the trigger. The crossbow twanged and the bolt flew almost faster than Jasmine could follow. The bolt punched into the barrel with a hollow thunk.

"This thing will take out a deader up to three hundred feet with these steel bolts, but only if you're lucky. The bolts are cobbed together from scrap and are not accurate. For you, don't shoot anything more than fifty feet away."

Cally handed the crossbow to Jasmine and picked out another bolt from a child's plastic sand bucket at her feet.

"Your turn," she said.

Jasmine put the crossbow on the ground and pulled the string back. Cally had made it look easy, but Jasmine thought her fingertips were going to fall off by the time she wrestled the string into the latch. She took the bolt from Cally and slid it back along the groove until it hit the string. She brought the weapon up and looked down the bolt toward the blue barrel.

"Hang on," Cally said.

Cally came up behind her and adjusted Jasmine's grip. She jerked the crossbow's stock hard into Jasmine's shoulder. Jasmine thought she heard something crunch in her shoulder joint.

"Hold it firm, but not tight."

What the hell was that supposed to mean? She'd ask later.

"Okay, fire when you're ready."

Jasmine took in a deep breath and looked over the bolt toward the blue barrel. Dangerous, she thought, I'm doing something dangerous. I'm holding a weapon, a killing thing. Her mouth felt dry. Stop it, Jas, you're just shooting a barrel. Pull the trigger.

She pulled the trigger. Nothing happened. Relief flowed through her as she lowered the weapon. This was a stupid idea anyway. She wasn't going to win any fights with this antiquated thing, just give herself tetanus.

"You left the safety on. Slide the button to the red dot."

"Maybe I should just stop."

"Honey, you're this far, you might as well shoot it at least once. I'm not out here to satisfy your highness's whims."

Highness? Jasmine hoisted the crossbow to her shoulder and thumbed off the safety. Damn, it was getting heavy! She sighted along the bolt.

"Hold it higher or you'll just hit dirt."

Jasmine lifted the crossbow.

"Higher. You gotta account for the drop."

Jasmine grunted and pushed the weapon's nose higher.

"Okay, fire."

Jasmine's finger reached for the trigger and pulled. The string twanged, and she felt the shock run through her arms. She watched the bolt leave, flying over the barrel into a pile of fiberglass panels and paint cans.

"What?" Jasmine said.

Cally sighed and pursed her lips.

"You closed your eyes and leaned back when you pulled the trigger."

"No I didn't."

Cally shrugged and nodded her head. Jasmine felt her face burn. It wasn't her fault, what could Cally expect from someone's first time? "I'll do better with the next one," Jasmine said and reached down for another bolt.

"No, Jas," Cally said.

"Huh?"

Cally pointed to the pile behind the barrel.

"Those bolts are a real bitch to make. Go find the one you shot before you forget where it landed."

It wasn't fair, Jasmine thought. How was she supposed to learn how to shoot if she spent her time searching for bolts? She got ready to heave the weapon at Cally. The woman lifted her chin and stared Jasmine down.

"Put it down gently, Jasmine. Crossbows are even harder to make than bolts."

"I quit."

"Honey, you can decide to quit on your own time, when it's just your ass on the line against everything out there. Right now, you're eating my food, sleeping under my roof, and enjoying the safety I provide. You make us less safe, okay? Today belongs to me. You will learn the basics of defending your-self out here or I will strip you naked and leave you for whatever comes knocking on the front gate. So put the crossbow down gently and go get the bolt."

Jasmine knelt and put the crossbow on the ground as slowly as she could. She gave it a little pat and plastered her sweetest smile on her face. Cally appeared untroubled.

"I don't care how long it takes you to do it, honey, as long as you do it."

She practiced for hours, until it seemed like her arms would fall off and her fingertips had been turned to hamburger. She had developed a little proficiency, able to hit the blue barrel seven out of ten times. That, plus a smoldering hatred of Cally, who sat in the shade swinging her feet and pointing out everything Jasmine was doing wrong. Too high, too low, not holding steady enough, and don't you dare lose a bolt, princess. She was beginning to really hate being called princess.

That night, she only had the energy to manage a weak smile as Bishop announced the Biscayne was running again. She ate quickly and left, falling to the couch in a heap. In her dreams, she endlessly fired the crossbow and watched the bolts veer off target into junk piles. Cally yelled at her to go pick them up but somehow she knew there were deaders waiting for her in the piles. She wanted to scream but was unable.

6

────────

Jasmine woke to the smell of barbecue: lighter fluid, smoke, and charred hamburgers. Someone had used too much lighter fluid though, and she hated it when her hamburgers tasted like gasoline.

Bishop ran through the room

"Get up, Jas, time to rock and roll!"

"When did we get hamburger, Bishop? You've been holding out on me."

Bishop didn't smile, he just stared down at her.

"Get your crossbow and come with me," he said.

Bishop sped down the hall, and Jasmine scrambled for the crossbow. She ran after Bishop, dodging piles of empty tin cans and holes in the floor. Bishop's feet thundered up the stairs to the roof. Gunfire erupted—the chatter of a machine gun.

Jasmine climbed through the trapdoor onto the roof. Cally stood in a pile of spent brass casings, sighting over the machine gun's barrel. Around the Love Shack, deaders illuminated by floodlights climbed the razor wire, oblivious to the strips of flesh left behind. They shambled down into the pits, crowded enough for others to walk on heads, shoulders, and backs to the next trench.

The machine gun fired again, Cally walking a line of bullets into deaders' torsos as they emerged. They fell back into the trenches, but more came crawling up the bank in their place. Cally stopped firing and calmly grabbed a new ammo belt.

"There's hundreds of them," Cally said.

"It ain't natural," Bishop said. "I've never seen a group this big."

"Me neither. Most I've had to deal with at once was a group of fifty, and that was just a bunch of smaller groups that happened to come at the same time."

Jasmine caught a flash from outside the fence, just beyond the floodlights' reach. She pointed.

"What's that?"

Bishop grabbed a pair of binoculars and looked into the darkness.

"Can't make it out."

A few deaders had made it to the inner ditches and started crossing.

"Allow me," Cally said. She turned and mashed a button built into a rusty metal box. Jasmine went blind for a moment as flame columns erupted. Every inch of exposed skin tightened as the heat hit her. Then the flames vanished, leaving clouds of oily smoke.

"Feel the foo, motherfuckers!" Cally yelled. The flaming deader remains shuddered in the pits. Jasmine looked away.

"Shit," Bishop said, taking the binoculars and handing them to Jasmine.

Jasmine looked out where she had seen the flash. Cally hit the flames again, and Jasmine saw the Blood Weeper straddling his motorcycle. He held his sword in one hand, resting its tip on the ground. Blood flowed down his cheeks. Deaders streamed around him toward the Love Shack. They paid him no mind, nor he them.

"We're dead," Jasmine said.

Cally fired another belt of ammunition into the deaders.

"What is it?" Cally asked.

"Kikuchiyo," Bishop said.

Cally pried apart the machine gun, laid in a new belt, and slammed it shut. "Why aren't the deaders eating him?"

Bishop shrugged and sighted down his rifle. "Maybe we can ask your boyfriend when we see him." He fired. A deader went down.

Jasmine looked around at the deaders filling the trenches. What should she do? She raised the crossbow to her shoulder and looked down the shaft at a deader wearing tattered leather pants and a single biker boot. She held her breath and reached for the trigger. Bishop caught her by the shoulder. He shouted in her ear over the machine gun fire.

"Save your ammo, babe. We're getting out of here. I'll get the car ready." He nodded at Cally. "You help her load so she can keep the area clear." He pointed to the ammo boxes around the parapet. "You've got enough here for about another five minutes." Jasmine nodded.

"When you're out, you run down to the car. Don't stop, okay?"

"Okay."

"Five minutes." He held up five fingers.

"Five."

Bishop nodded once then leaned in and kissed her on the mouth. Jasmine reached up to push him away, but he was already gone.

"Ammo," Cally said.

"He kissed me," Jasmine said.

"Be glad he didn't grab your ass. Ammo!"

Jasmine put her crossbow down and wrenched open an ammo box.

"Bring it over here!" Cally said.

Jasmine picked the box up, the muscles in her back straining. She dropped it next to Cally.

"Turn it around. Pointy ends toward the barrel."

Jasmine turned the box so the bullets faced the way Cally wanted. She handed the belt up to Cally. The woman grabbed it and closed the machine gun. The muzzle flared with orange-white flashes as Cally sent a burst into some deaders caught up on razor wire.

"This is my house," Cally yelled, punctuating her words with short bursts from the gun. "My. Fucking. House."

She swung the barrel back and forth, taking out pockets of deaders with short, controlled bursts.

"Ammo!"

Jasmine ran and got another box of bullets. Her eyes stung with smoke and the hot sting of gunpowder filled her head. She managed to bring the ammo box back and get it oriented in the right direction. Cally was firing again in seconds. How much time had passed? It seemed like an hour but couldn't have been more than a few seconds.

"Fire in the hole!"

Cally punched the button and the night glowed orange as the foo jets ignited. Burning limbs fell away as the deaders continued to climb the trench's walls.

"Shoot the Blood Weeper. Maybe the deaders will stop if we kill him."

"Bullets don't do anything to the Weeper except get him mad," Cally said.

"He's already mad. Can it hurt to try?"

"As a matter of fact, it can. Shut up." Cally pulled back a bolt and began firing.

Jasmine closed her mouth only because shouting over the machine gun fire would accomplish nothing. She turned away and started stacking ammo boxes closer to the gun. Maybe it saved a few seconds, but she couldn't stand and do nothing. Cally fired her bursts and screamed at the deaders, pausing only to shout "Ammo!" and fire the foo jets when the inner trenches were in danger of being overrun. Jasmine knew she should be scared, but the work of keeping the machine gun fed focused her. Soon Jasmine noticed they were down to the last ammo box.

"Last one," Jasmine called out.

Cally slammed the machine gun shut and worked the bolt. She raised the barrel out toward the perimeter.

"This one's for you, Kikuchiyo!" she said, and fired a long burst, sweeping the barrel back and forth.

Jasmine saw something sparkle out beyond the flood lights and heard a guttural yell. The Blood Weeper stepped into the light, sword before him in both hands. Cally walked the machine gun fire straight at him, and Jasmine saw the sparks surround the samurai as he batted bullets aside with his blade. Some bullets ricocheted into the thinning stream of deaders, knocking them down. Then the last of the ammo belt disappeared into the gun and the firing stopped. The Blood Weeper lowered his sword. Blood still streamed from his eyes, but he appeared unhurt. He roared and swung his sword around in an arc, cutting through three deaders as if they were made of air. They toppled to the ground, torsos in pieces.

"Now he's mad," Cally said.

"I thought that was a bad idea."

"That was then. Now, I want him close."

"You what?"

Cally mashed the foo jets one more time. Jasmine saw the Blood Weeper running straight at them, cutting away at the deaders in his path. Then the heavy foo smoke obscured everything.

"Time to go, honey," Cally said. She grabbed Jasmine by the hand and scooped up the crossbow. She pushed the weapon into Jasmine's arms and pushed her toward the stairs.

As Jasmine ran down the corridors, her ragged breathing and pounding heart filled her ears. She wove her way around the garbage heaps and metal fuel drums. She turned left, right, left again. She heard shouts outside, metal screeching. Was she supposed to turn left or right after the third bedroom? She couldn't remember. She stopped, not recognizing anything around her. Cally had disappeared. How could that bitch abandon her?

Downstairs, wood cracked like thunder. The front door. The Love Shack's floor plan righted itself in her head and she ran in the opposite direction. Several turns later, she came to the narrow stairwell leading down. She took it in two bounds, thankful for young knees that absorbed the shock without complaint. She heard scrambling behind the door leading into the kitchen and peeked inside.

Two deaders, one in black leather, the other in a leopard-print cocktail dress, pawed through the cabinets, dumping cans on the floor. She felt the urge to back away and take the other door through to the back porch, but she stayed rooted to the floor. The deaders seemed more upset with each can they found, working faster until they were like moles digging through loose sand. The one in black leather stopped and came away with a box of crackers. It ripped the package open, sending crackers flying. It stuffed a handful into its mouth. The other deader came over and reached for the package, only to have it pulled away. The two fought over the box, Black Leather fending off Leopard-print with one hand and stuffing crackers in its mouth with the other. Bits of dried flesh came away in their hands, but they didn't seem to slow. Then Leopard-print noticed her.

It got to its feet and came for her. Black Leather rose, leaving the smashed crackers behind.

"Hasssstt," Leopard-print said and reached out for her.

Jasmine raised the crossbow and fired. The bolt took the deader in the chest, and it toppled over. Black Leather rushed forward, stumbling over its companion. Jasmine found her feet and ran, slamming the kitchen door behind her.

She jumped off the back porch and sprinted past the rusted metal barricades to the Biscayne. Bishop had already started the car and was waving her in the back seat.

"Where's Cally?"

"I don't know, we got separated. We gotta go."

"We wait."

"There are already deaders in there, and she got the samurai angry. I think he broke down the front door."

"Get in the back seat. We'll wait."

"We'll die if we stay."

Bishop shrugged. "If we don't wait for Cally, we'll die anyway."

Jasmine muttered to herself and crawled over the front seat, pushing a box of cans to the side and wedging herself into the back seat. She pushed her legs into the gaps between blue plastic water jugs at her feet and wiped at the dusty window beside her. Where was the handle for rolling the window down? A deader appeared, clambering around a pile of bedsprings. This one wore a popped collar and skinny tie with the remains of a grey business suit.

"Bishop," Jasmine said, scrambling for a crossbow bolt.

The deader's head blew apart. The body toppled forward as Cally rounded the corner, shotgun in hand.

"You coming, Cally, or should I drive around the block a few times first?"

"I had to get my favorite shoes," she said and slid into the passenger seat.

"Your shoes?" Jasmine said. "With a sword-wielding maniac loose in the house?'

"I wasn't going to leave them for *him* to wear, honey." She looked at her watch. "Thirty seconds, let's go."

Bishop nodded and put the Biscayne in gear. As the car eased around the junk piles, Jasmine looked behind them. More deaders came around the corner, a few stopping to gnaw at their dead comrade.

"Deaders behind us," Jasmine said.

"Don't worry about them," Bishop said. "Look out for ones in front and nail 'em if you can."

"But the ones back there will catch up."

"I wouldn't worry about it."

"Looks serious to me," Jasmine said.

Cally rested her shotgun's barrel on the windowsill. "Honey, in fifteen seconds, it ain't gonna matter."

"In our slow-motion getaway?" Coming in, it had taken them forever to negotiate the wooden planks over the trenches. Those planks were gone now. She glanced behind them. The mob was back on its feet. They shambled a few steps forward, then shuddered. The front row parted as the samurai came running through, sword in hand.

"Blood Weeper!"

"See him," Bishop said.

"Five seconds," Cally said.

Bishop eased around the last junk pile and straightened the wheel. There was no plank bridge, no way the car could get over the trench. Deaders crawled onto the front bumper. Cally leaned out and fired a few shotgun blasts into their chests, knocking them back. Bishop reached across the seat and pulled her back in. Then the earth exploded.

Geysers of earth reached into the night sky around them, radiating outward in a deep rumbling syncopation. Bodies and earth flew in the air and bits pelted the roof like hail. Jasmine covered her head and closed her eyes. Being buried alive was not the way she wanted to go out. Suffocation would get her before she died of thirst. She couldn't breathe already. She sucked in deep breaths, trying to capture what little oxygen was left, but there wasn't enough. Her lungs burned. She was thrown back in her seat. Another explosion? The windows went black. Jasmine tried holding her breath. Then the earth lurched again, and the sky glowed orange.

Pulverized dirt, gravel, rusty metal, and body parts surrounded them. The trenches had disappeared, and the Biscayne headed toward the front gate, slewing from side to side as Bishop fought for traction. In the corner of her eye, the Love Shack became a pillar of flame hundreds of feet high, slowly collapsing into itself. Heat pulled at her skin through the window. They passed the front gate and roared away as wheels caught asphalt.

Cally sighed.

"Party's finally over," she said.

"What the hell was all that?"

"Cally's escape plan. While you ran your ass back to the car, Cally armed the detonators on some buried foo barrels."

"Some?" Jasmine said.

"Something like six hundred, I'd guess," Bishop said.

"I had a lot of time on my hands while waiting for Ryan. I kept myself busy, came up with some stuff."

"Like sequenced charges that could clear a route for a quick getaway by car," Bishop said.

"Yeah, and I tied in the reserves too. A parting fuck-you for Kikuchiyo, the asshole."

She looked back at the glowing horizon and let out a ragged breath. Bishop reached over and gripped her hand.

"Sorry," he said.

Cally shook her head. "We had so many good times in that place."

"But at least we got the Blood Weeper," Jasmine said.

"Nah. We just delayed him a bit," Bishop said.

"There's no way he could have survived all that," Jasmine said.

"He's survived worse. I just hope we get enough of a head start to stay ahead."

Cally's eyes glistened. Jasmine shifted around in the back seat, trying unsuccessfully to find a comfortable position. Bishop turned the Biscayne onto the highway and stomped on the gas, pushing Jasmine's shoulder into an unyielding wooden crate. Cally leaned her head on the window glass and sniffed.

"You're better off," Jasmine said, fighting her way forward. "That place was a dump. Ryan probably would have thought it was abandoned anyway."

Cally whipped around and her hand snapped out, catching Jasmine across the face.

"Shut up, princess. You don't have the first clue."

Jasmine rubbed at her cheek. Princess? Ryan's girlfriends had never gotten the best of her, and this one wasn't going to be the first.

"Really? A falling down shack in the middle of a junkyard that stinks like an oil refinery? Yeah, what a palace."

"It was the safest place in the Badlands," Cally said, "A goddamn fortress."

"So damn safe, a zombie army led by a bulletproof samurai walked right in. Fat lot of good all the guns, pits, and fire did. It's all useless junk now. Bishop's right, we gotta stay moving."

"Keep me out of this," Bishop said.

Cally waved a hand in Jasmine's face. "What are you going to do, run forever? Please. Nothing ever made it to the front door until you showed up. And you're welcome, by the way, for letting you in and saving your sorry ass with all my useless junk so Bishop could get the car working."

Jasmine stared, knowing Cally was right, but she couldn't bring herself to thank her. The silence stretched out.

"You're an ungrateful useless little bitch, you know that?" Cally said and smiled.

"You're a homeless slut, waiting for someone who will never come," Jasmine said, smiling back.

Jasmine saw the words hit home. Cally's smile tightened as she turned back to Bishop.

"I guess I'll have to find him myself now, won't I? Ryan, I mean. If he came back tomorrow, he'd probably think I was dead."

"Don't worry about it," Bishop said.

"Why?" Cally said.

Bishop chewed the inside of his cheek for a moment, then nodded.

"Because we're going to light the towers and make our way to Paradise City."

Cally squealed and half-leaned, half-pulled herself to plant a kiss on Bishop's cheek.

"What does that mean?" Jasmine said.

Cally turned, beaming. "It means we're going to follow the lights to Paradise."

7

———————

Cally sang along with the radio, some song about a woman's phone number. Her right arm was stuck out the window, porpoising up and down in the car's slipstream. In another variation from real-world Kelly, Cally's singing voice was clear and perfectly pitched, with an ethereal quality that would make angels weep. Bishop tapped his finger against the steering wheel in time to the music.

Jasmine stared at the back of their heads. Her back screamed from loading ammo boxes, and her knees ached from not being able to put her feet on the floor. Her Keds rested on a box filled with unlabeled tin cans.

"Come on, Bishop," Jasmine said, "Can't we turn the radio off?"

Bishop glanced at her in the rearview mirror. "Shotgun's in charge of the radio."

"Then pull over so we can switch."

"Not until later."

"Well, at least let me stretch out back here. My legs are killing me."

Bishop shook his head. "Stay buckled in."

"What, are we expecting traffic? We're the only ones on the road."

"Stay buckled in," Bishop said.

Jasmine sat back, disgusted. She looked out the window. Endless sand, brush, and rock. Just like the last hundred miles. The sun tracked down on the horizon; it would be dark soon.

Cally nodded her head in time to the music as she sang. Jasmine felt pity for her. She was just a teenage fantasy made flesh, and not even an original. Even in idealized form she was still a slut, even if she couldn't help it. Ignorance is no excuse, after all.

"My knees hurt. Can't we stop for just a minute?"

"Wah wah, wah wah-wah," Cally said. She pouted and traced an imaginary tear down her face with a fingertip.

"Play nice girls. It's a long trip."

Cally smiled. "Oh I always play nice. Especially with her brother. He had the cutest little ass you ever did see."

"Shut up," Jasmine said.

"And I saw a lot of it. Did you know we had a mirror above our bed? Not a big one, but just big enough to see that cute ass of his moving up and down, up and down."

"Stop it, Cally," Jasmine said. Her stomach churned as images of her brother's naked butt came to her unbidden, Cally's face looking over Ryan's shoulder and laughing.

"Thrusting and thrusting until my eyes rolled back in my head, and I'd scream!" She let out a note that threatened to break the windows.

Jasmine pushed Cally with both hands. "That's enough!" she said, but Cally just laughed.

"Oh come on. You'd deny your brother a little sex just because you've never done it? You prude!"

"You don't know anything about me."

"You remind me of that song, *Like a Virgin*. It just pops into my head every time I see you." She tapped a finger against her chin. "I wonder why that is?"

Jasmine's first time was at fifteen with Kai Miller. She doubted that information would help. She racked her brain for something to put Cally in her place. "Slut" was all that came out.

"Cut it out, Cally," Bishop said.

Cally put on a look like she was hurt, but she couldn't keep a malicious grin from her face. "Sure, take her side. Just because she's never been laid it's okay for her to get all bitchy. Maybe you could do us all a favor and screw her tonight so she'll loosen up."

Jasmine reached out and grabbed two handfuls of hair. She pulled Cally toward the head rest as hard as she could. Cally's nails dug into the back of Jasmine's hands.

"Lemme go, bitch," Cally said.

"How's this for loosening up, skank?" Jasmine said. She yanked Cally's head to the headrest again.

Brakes squealed, and they both flew forward. Jasmine's nose struck the head rest, just short of re-aggravating the break from before, thanks to the seatbelt. Cally's head avoided smacking against the dashboard for the same reason.

The car became quiet but for the sound of the idling engine. Bishop's hands were locked on the wheel, and his jaw worked against the side of his cheek. Ten seconds passed before he spoke.

"I don't need this crap right now. I don't want to hear this crap right now," He turned to face them. "If I hear more crap like this, I'm gonna lock you both in the trunk and turn the radio up real loud so I won't have to hear crap like this anymore. Got it?"

Jasmine drew in a breath to protest, but Bishop cocked his head to the side and gave her a look that almost dared her to say something. He gave his head a sharp turn and gave the same look to Cally. No one said anything.

"Good," Bishop said. He put the car in gear and started down the road.

THEY STOPPED JUST AFTER DUSK. Bishop got them all out and set up a quick camp while Cally kept watch with her shotgun. Jasmine didn't know how to help. When she offered to go get firewood, Bishop shook his head and said it was too dangerous for her to go out. Better to stay with Cally and the car while he went, he said. She made herself busy putting together a fire ring from rocks, ignoring Cally as the woman walked a perimeter humming 80s tunes. Jasmine offered to start the fire when Bishop came back and asked for the matches. Cally let out a loud laugh. Bishop instead showed her how to get a spark from a flint, but she only managed to scrape up her knuckles. Bishop smiled and gently but firmly took the flint and strike from her hands. He said she could try again tomorrow.

Dinner was a shared can of tuna and refried beans, which Jasmine ate without complaint. Everything was washed down with warm over-chlorinated water. Cally was all laughs and perky banter with Bishop and even tried to get Jasmine talking as though nothing had happened earlier. Jasmine kept her responses short and tried to avoid eye contact.

"Well," Bishop said after the food was finished, "with a bit of luck, we won't run out of food before we find Paradise City."

"Find? I thought you knew how to get there," Cally said. "What the hell were we driving all afternoon for?"

"It ain't all that simple," Bishop said with a sigh. "Look, it's like this. The city isn't exactly in what you call a fixed location. You need to move with it if you want to find it."

Cally's eyebrows worked together. "How the hell do we do that?"

"Like I said, we'll need to light the first beacon."

"And what the hell is a beacon?"

"There are radio towers all over this place. If we power up the grid, the towers in line with Paradise City will light up. So we find the first beacon, switch on the power, and climb up. From there we can get a direction on the next one."

"That's stupid," Jasmine said.

Bishop shrugged. "Your brother thought it was a cool idea."

"Why do we have to climb up, can't we just follow them along the road?"

Bishop shook his head. "No, there's hills and stuff in the way between them. You need a clear shot to know which direction to go next."

"Paradise City, here we come," Cally said. She got a far off look in her eye. "It's got dance halls, live bands, cold beer, green grass, and everything." She stroked the shotgun in her arms absently like a cat. "I've always wanted to see it."

"And it moves," Jasmine said. "How?"

"You'll see," Bishop said.

They cleaned up the camp, though Jasmine didn't see the point. This place was a wasteland anyway, why worry about a few cans

"You sure we got enough food to get there?" Cally asked. Jasmine wasn't certain, but she thought Cally glanced in her direction.

"It'll be tight with all three of us, but we should manage," Bishop said.

"But what if it isn't?" Cally asked.

"Then we'll figure out something else," Bishop said. He went around the car, inspecting it and rubbing his hands over the surfaces. He popped the hood and looked at the engine.

Jasmine looked around at the red rocks and dead bushes, wondering when they last saw rain. Cally paced around with the shotgun, seemingly without a care in the world, but her eyes scanned constantly, missing nothing. Her feet automatically avoided the rocks that would otherwise trip her. She was as at home here as a lioness in the savannah, perfectly adapted to her environment. Jasmine felt like a poodle. What good was she to these people? Who would be left on the roadside when the food ran out? She needed to pull her own weight, she realized. Cally wouldn't hesitate to leave her.

She watched Bishop work his way around the engine. How much had he risked saving her? If she had anything like a friend here, it was him. She remembered the feel of his lips on hers. It had surprised her, but it hadn't been too bad. Not that she was going to let it happen again, of course, but she could at least be a little friendly.

She joined Bishop under the hood.

"What are you doing?"

Bishop grunted as he twisted at a knob. "Making sure this thing won't fail on us." The knob came free and he held it up to his eyes, checking the fluid level on the built-in dipstick.

"Can I help?"

"That depends, babe. How much you know about engines?"

"Nothing, really."

"Then no."

"So teach me. How big is this engine?"

"Four twenty-seven V-eight," he said, "With a four-speed Hurst shifter." He twisted the knob back on and plunged his hands back into the engine's innards.

"Is that a lot?" She felt stupid for asking, but she had to start somewhere, right?

"It's enough." He pulled out the dipstick. A thick oil droplet threatened to plummet from the end.

Jasmine tried to put on a charming smile. "What's the fastest you've ever gone in it?"

"Don't know," Bishop said. He turned the dipstick around, peering at the marks.

"What do you mean, you don't know?" All the guys Jasmine knew could not only tell you how fast they'd gone in their cars, but also what road, mile marker, and whether or not there was a girl involved.

"Speedometer's broken."

"It must have worked sometime."

"Nope, not ever." He put the dipstick back and wiped his hand on his jeans.

"So you have to check the oil. I can do that easy enough. What else do we do?"

Bishop looked at her over his sunglasses. "We do nothing. I don't let anyone else work on my car, okay?"

"I want to help."

"Then stay out of the way."

"I helped you fix this thing at the Love Shack."

"You handed me tools. That's not fixing a car."

"So give me lessons or something."

Bishop swept his arm across the engine. "This is the engine, the heart of the Biscayne. If something goes wrong, we're all fucked. With me so far?"

Jasmine rolled her eyes. "Yeah."

Bishop held up his bandaged hand.

"This is what happens when I trust you with something important. No way am I letting you do this to my car." He reached up and slammed the hood down. "Lesson's over. Time to go find our beacon."

THE BISCAYNE'S headlights bounced up and down as they navigated the gravel road. The dust kicked up, making the outer edges of the hi-beams visible in the grayness. Bishop turned the lights down, but Jasmine still had problems making out shapes in the night.

A structure emerged as they rounded a bend. Bishop and Cally seemed excited, but all Jasmine could see as they pulled up was a brick building no bigger than a closet.

"Who's ready for a trip to Paradise City?" Bishop said.

Cally bounced in her seat and raised her hand. "Oh, oh! Me! Me!"

"How about you, babe?"

Jasmine just looked back at him.

"I guess the honor is yours, Cally." Bishop reached into a pocket in the sun visor and tossed her a key. Cally beamed and jumped out. She unlocked the door to the closet and reached inside. She faced the car and flourished with her free arm.

"Ladies and Gentlemen, it is with great honor that I light our way to Paradise," Cally said. "Ten ... nine ... eight ..."

Jasmine leaned out the window. "Just do it, we don't have all night."

Cally stuck out her tongue and threw an unseen switch. On a rise behind her, several lights came to life with a pop, illuminating a radio tower that now glowed with a red light on top.

The light blinked in the darkness in an almost lazy manner. On for a second, then a slow fade to off, then off for a moment, and back on. Oddly, it relaxed Jasmine, providing some order and predictability to the area. Then again, it also marked the source of the day's horrible radio music.

"It's beautiful, isn't it?" Cally said as she got in the Biscayne. Bishop pulled back onto the gravel path toward the tower.

"You mean that's it? Big deal."

"Then you can climb it," Bishop said. "I don't like heights."

"What, me? Forget it. I don't do heights either. Cally?"

"I faint if I climb on a chair. Let's vote. Everyone in favor of sending Jasmine say 'aye.'"

Bishop said, "Aye."

Jasmine leaned forward in her seat. "Wait a minute, I thought you said you couldn't trust me. I don't know anything about this place. I'll get us all lost."

Bishop shrugged and turned the wheel. The beacon disappeared as the road switched back on itself. "Cally and I will stay down and keep an eye out for deaders. Just climb up and point your finger at the next beacon. You can manage that."

She couldn't make fire, find food, fix a car, drive fast, or in any other way keep them alive. If she wanted to start pulling her weight, she'd have to start somewhere. Fine.

"Fine," Jasmine said.

A chain-link fence materialized out of the dust cloud, the gate hanging open on broken hinges. As the Biscayne passed, the gravel gave way to cracked pavement with dead, waist-high grass poking though.

They drove up to the tower, which seemed a lot taller as she got closer. Intellectually, she knew it should be fine. There wasn't much rust on the ladder, and thick steel cables supported the structure on three sides, each cable sunk into massive concrete blocks that looked to be in better shape than the road.

But Jasmine still felt the butterflies stirring within her. The red light on top seemed ominous now, a warning to stay away. The wind picked up and the tower creaked, sending a panic spasm down her spine.

"Forget it. I'm not going."

Bishop looked up. "Yup, it's mighty high up there. Tell you what, you stay down here with Cally and try not to say anything that might make her shoot you. I'll go up there and see if my left hand has enough strength to hang onto the rung. I'm sure if I slip, everything will work out." He looked at Jasmine with a mild expression on his face. "What do you think?"

Jasmine felt the heat rise in her cheeks and was glad it was dark. "Can't we send Cally instead?"

"Maybe, I'm sure her high heels and fear of heights won't trouble her much. You can stay down here where it's safe." He cocked his head to the side as if in thought. "That is unless there's a deader around, or a psycho samurai."

"Fine. I'll go, but don't expect me to fly up the ladder."

"Just find the next tower and let me know which way it is. I'll figure it out from there."

"Without a map?"

Bishop tapped his head. "All in here."

"Okay, wish me luck," she said.

"Break a leg," Cally said. She just smiled at Jasmine's glare.

The first twenty feet weren't so bad. Then the wind picked up again. A creak raced through the tower's skeleton and through her body. She closed her eyes and waited for the wind to die down. That turned out to be a mistake, because with her eyes closed she could feel the tower's sway as the wind whistled by. She opened her eyes, but the swaying sensation remained. Bishop called up to her, and she resisted the urge to look down, knowing she'd fail for sure if she did. She advanced to the next rung, which seemed to make Bishop happy; he stopped yelling anyway.

It seemed to take hours, just focusing on putting one hand a rung farther up and willing her body to follow. She settled into a rhythm of right foot push, right hand grab, left hand grab, left foot catch up, and breathe. She stared at her hands for the most part, stealing glances every three rungs to see if she had reached the top. The beacon loomed larger in her vision and her world alternated between being bathed in red light and plummeted into complete darkness.

She knew she was getting to the end when she could hear the beacon humming, pitching higher as the light brightened and lowering to a drone as it went dark. It was like sneaking up on a giant heart or a sleeping dragon. The wind howled and she froze on the ladder until it slowed. Finally, she placed her hand on the last rung. She let out her breath and looked out across the wasteland. There was nothing but darkness.

"No way," she whispered to herself. She turned her head into the wind as it picked up, her hands gripping the rungs with a death-grip. The whistling in her ears was like a banshee wail, and her buffeted eyes watered. She caught a glimpse of the ground and the little box of the Biscayne. The world seemed to turn under her and she felt herself falling. Her hands ached on the rungs, and she spun around until her forehead rested against the cold metal ladder. She wasn't falling. Vertigo. Must be vertigo. The afterimages faded from her vision.

Wait, there was something in the corner of her eye. Something in the afterimage that didn't fit. She opened her eyes and turned again. There, just peeking above the dark shape of a mesa, a red light winked in the dark. Bishop wanted her to point it out to him, but she didn't think he could see her from the ground. She turned back to the ladder, fixed the distant tower in her head, then stuck her hand out and pointed where she thought it was. When she opened her eyes, a red light blinked just over her fingertip. She repeated the exercise twice more so she wouldn't forget. She was not coming up here again.

The trip down was, if anything, harder than the trip up. Every step was a potential slip, her hands went numb, and her forearms burned. When her foot finally touched the ground, she let go and collapsed to her back, staring back up the ladder to the distant red light. Bishop's hand grabbed her by the wrist and pulled her to her feet.

"Which way?"

She placed one hand on the ladder, swung her arm, and pointed. "That way."

"You sure?" he said.

"Go up your damn self and check it if you don't believe me."

He grinned. "All right, let's go."

Jasmine's reward for finding the next beacon was day watch while Bishop and Cally slept in the car. The deaders weren't necessarily nocturnal, but it was a lot harder to shamble unnoticed in the daylight. Jasmine sat in the shade of the car holding Cally's shotgun. (It's pretty much the same as the crossbow and the boom will wake us up, but don't waste any ammo okay, princess?) Cally snored. With all the changes Ryan had made in Cally, why he had left that in her, Jasmine couldn't figure out.

Jasmine kicked at a rock. Her shoes and shorts had taken on a pinkish hue, saturated by the ubiquitous red dust. She pulled out her ponytail and combed at her hair with her fingers. It was getting a little stringy. She was getting BO as fragrant as the others too. She didn't notice the odor all the time, but sometimes the smell reasserted itself as a rank, musky, and much too feral stench for her to accept as normal. She added a bath to her running wish list.

She got up and walked around, making sure nothing approached. The air stirred, and a small swirling dust devil danced across her path. Was it an omen or just the wasteland mocking her? She watched the devil evaporate and shook her head.

"You think too much, Jas," she said to herself. That was always her problem, thinking things over and over again, getting locked into an endless cycle until something bad happened to break her out of it. If she had known life ended with a trip to a place like this, would she have killed herself? Would it have made any difference?

"Kill yourself and end up in hell." She muttered. Her shirt was sweat-plastered to her back again. Bishop had warned her not to exert herself too much, as they didn't have water to waste. She wanted to tell him it wouldn't matter anyway. Whether or not Ryan still lived on this hell, plane, or whatever it was called, he made the rules. He abandoned this place and by extension, her. If he had really wanted her to see him, why not put the tree house somewhere closer to Paradise City?

She heard a cry above her and held a hand out to shield her eyes from the sun. A bird circled high overhead. Must be waiting for her to drop dead. If she did, would the bird survive a bit longer? Wouldn't that be a good thing? She had brought a tree back to life, after all.

Had she really? She had handled plenty of dead plants at the Love Shack, and none had come back to life. What was different about the tree? She stopped and thought about it. She had picked up the can, cut her finger, and ... what? Had the tree gotten a drop of her blood? The Love Shack's carpet certainly got enough when Cally rammed the shotgun's butt in her face, and nothing happened. But that was a building, a made thing, and had never been alive. Maybe that made a difference.

"Only one way to find out," she said. She walked back to the Biscayne and gently took the machete out from the car seat scabbard as Cally snored away. She walked to a tiny bush, a twisted brown thing that could have been juniper or poison oak for all she knew. But it had lived at one time, and it was small. Perhaps it wouldn't take as long to see results.

She sat cross-legged with the machete balanced on her knees. Flecks of rust and unidentifiable stains coated the flat of the blade, only the very edge showed gleaming metal. Did she have the tetanus vaccine in this body? What about hepatitis?

"Quit thinking, just do it," she said. She ran her thumb against the blade's heel, assuming it was the sharpest and least likely part to be carrying any pathogens or other nasty surprises. A quick flash of pain, and her thumb bled.

She reached out and rubbed the bush's stem. She was rewarded with another stab of pain as a tiny thorn wedged itself in the cut.

"Ungrateful bastard," she said. She picked the thorn out and sucked at the cut. Gotta stop making this a habit, she thought, or else people will think something's wrong with you. The idea struck her funny enough to make her mouth crinkle into a smile.

She wrapped the thumb in a black bandanna she had borrowed from Bishop. She put the machete to the side and waited. If it worked, what then? Bleed over anything needing a new life? Open an artery and spray it around like a garden sprinkler?

Chances were it wouldn't work anyway and she was just self-mutilating. Nothing wrong with that if you were in rock and roll and could get paid for it. Otherwise, they called the crisis hotline on you. Counseling, interventions, little old ladies telling you what to do, where you went wrong. They'd seize on Ryan's death and nod their heads sagely and say "of course, there's the source of all this troubled young girl's problems."

That's why she had wanted to do a proper job of killing herself. No botched attempts. She was sure most failed suicides wanted the attention of getting caught. She just wanted to be left alone.

She placed her fingertips on the bush after checking for thorns. Was it was vibrating or just moving with the wind? She wondered if she should have picked something bigger. Why the hell had Ryan created this plant anyway? If he made this place, why not make the bushes grow something more useful, like cranberries or something? She could go for some cranberries right now, and some turkey to go with it. Rolls, sweet potato pie, and coffee. Goddamn, she missed coffee.

Her stomach roiled, so she went back to thinking about Ryan. Maybe he couldn't control everything. Maybe this stuff happened automatically, subconsciously, or was somehow already around when he got here. The thought chilled her. If her subconscious had power like that, they'd probably find the highway littered with copies of the white high-top sneakers Ryan had worn the night he died.

She had fought to see the pictures from the accident, denied by her parents, then the police, but she had won in the end. The very first picture she saw was a black-and-white photo of his left sneaker lying where the pavement gave way to the gravel shoulder. The rest of him had been found in the ditch, knocked clear out of his shoes. For the next couple of years, the image repeated itself in her dreams. Bloody high-tops and something scary in the long grass along the ditch. She would wake in a sweat if she were lucky. If she were unlucky, she would find herself rooted to the pavement while a pickup crested the hill behind her. She would be bathed in light as it swerved first toward her, then away but too late. She would then fly through the air toward the ditch. Ryan would be there waiting for her in the long grass, blood smeared his face, his hair, his clothes. His chest would appear collapsed on one side, like it had melted. He would open his arms for an embrace, and only when she was a breath away from landing would she wake up.

The bush started quivering. She could feel tiny tremors through her legs, not the powerful thrumming the oak had made but something quicker, like a rabbit's pulse. The whole bush shook, casting the last dry leaves to the ground. Then it turned green where she had touched it with her bloody thumb, a rich lime green she always associated with the shoots of the first spring tulips. It spread throughout the bush, creating leaves along its branches. New growth started at the tips, adding almost two full inches along the branches. The quivering subsided, but then gave one last effort. Buds appeared and burst into broad-petaled flowers, pink at the centers giving way to pure white at the tips. They filled the air with a scent cleaner than soap.

It was beautiful. It scared the hell out of her.

～

THE THREE OF them stood around the bush in silence. Cally looked at Jasmine with a kind of awe in her eyes; Bishop seemed scared. Jasmine didn't know which reaction troubled her the most. The bush didn't wilt or seem to be in any way affected by the dry air and scorching sun. The waxy leaves had turned a dark green and swayed in the breeze while the flowers continued to pump out their fresh scent to lure whatever life remained.

"It's so beautiful," Cally said. "I mean I've heard of flowers in the desert before, but this is just amazing." She turned and put her arms around Jasmine. "And you did it, Jas, you've brought beauty back to us."

Jasmine did her best to endure the touch from the slut with the runny mascara. Anything to avoid another broken nose.

"It's goddamn impossible," Bishop said, walking around the bush. "Unnatural even."

"Thanks for not making me feel like a complete freak," Jasmine said. Her voice cracked as she said it, which resulted in a squeeze from Cally.

"Leave her alone, Bishop. This is a miracle, she can save us all, can't you see?"

Bishop reached out with a finger and stroked a leaf. His whole body seemed coiled, like he was waiting for a signal to run or strike out. "Will she? I don't know." He looked up at Jasmine. "So this is what happened to the oak tree?"

"Yeah."

"A whole tree?" Cally said. She gave a little jump, anchored to the ground only because she refused to release Jasmine from her embrace. Jasmine stumbled. "Why didn't you say something earlier? Can you do other things, like make it rain and stuff?" Cally's eyes were burning with a sense of awe so strong Jasmine imagined she would believe anything without question.

"How about it, Jasmine," Bishop said, "Can you do anything else?" He said it mildly, but Jasmine could hear the weight he gave the words, like the next words from her mouth should be carefully chosen.

"I don't know. I haven't tried anything else, I'm not even sure what this means. I'm just as confused as you are." She looked right into his eyes, still hiding behind the sunglasses. She saw her reflection in them, a skinny teenager wearing a human-shaped yellow backpack. She gently pried Cally's arms away and squatted down to Bishop's level. She met her own gaze in the dark glasses for a moment before she had to look away.

"The only thing I'm sure of is that it scares the hell out of me," she said.

"Me too, kid."

He stood up and brushed the dust off his pants. He froze before the dust cloud settled.

"Everybody stay cool," he said in a quiet voice. "Very carefully, we're going to the car. Do not run, do not look around."

"What?" Cally said. Her eyes had grown large and were looking all around, but her body had not moved.

"Deaders, about fifty yards out."

Jasmine's heart clenched in her chest. So close, sneaking up while they were distracted. And on her watch, she realized.

"How many?"

"Too many to fight," Bishop said. "But we can get away if we go now and don't spook them." He reached out a hand to Jasmine and pulled her up. "Now on three, two, one, go."

Jasmine turned around and her breath caught in her throat. A line of about twenty shambling bodies approached, emaciated and dotted with scabs. Black, white, brown, men, women, and at least two children shuffle-stepped toward them. The wind carried their scent to her now, a rancid odor like rotten meat.

Bishop put a hand on each girl's shoulder and the three walked to the Biscayne. "Haaaaa-sssssss-hhaaaaaah," whispered on the wind.

"Do you hear?" Cally said.

"Just keep walking," Bishop said, whispering.

"But they've never talked before."

"Shh," Bishop said. They had made it about halfway to the car, the open doors looking to Jasmine like water in a desert. She forced herself to put one foot in front of the other at Bishop's agonizing pace. Everything in her fiber screamed to run. Bishop's hand held her in check. Her pounding heart and the deaders' whispering chant filled her ears, growing louder with every step.

"Sister!" Cally whispered. "They're saying 'sister, sister.'" She looked at Jasmine in horror. "They're calling for you, Jas. They know who you are."

Jasmine lurched from Bishop's grip. Her vision narrowed, and all she could see were the car doors. There were shouts all around, and a sound like dead leaves on pavement. Her legs pumped and time slowed down. The car was fifteen feet away, ten, five. She jumped in and pulled the far door shut. Her hand slammed down on the lock. She reached behind her and pulled the driver's door shut, locking it as soon as it slammed home.

Bishop and Cally slammed their palms on the glass, calling her name. On the other side, a toothless face leered at her. Another appeared, and another. They scratched at the windows, pulled at the door. Jasmine curled into herself, bringing her knees up to her chin.

"Jasmine! Jasmine! Open it! Open! Open open!"

"Sssssss-haaaa-Sssssss-haaaa."

"Just go away," she whispered as the tears rolled down her face. "Leave me alone." She stared straight ahead, no longer able to look at the flesh pressing on either side. Something pounded on the window, once, twice. A crash. Glass broke. Tiny pieces pelted her cheek and fell to the floor like shiny pebbles. A door opened, and she was knocked down. Something raked at her shoulder, and she screamed.

The engine started, and she was thrown to the floor as the Biscayne lurched forward. Dirt, rock, and sand hissed against the underbody. There were two quick thumps against the side, then three bumps that bounced her head against the underside of the glove box, and then nothing. Just the Biscayne's roar and the smooth hum of pavement.

She looked up into Cally's blue eyes. Then everything went blurry and the tears came again. Sobs racked her chest, and she felt gentle hands pull her off the floor and onto the seat. Two arms wrapped themselves around her and rocked her. Cally smelled of stale sweat and gunpowder, but she felt warm. Cally hummed a tune Jasmine couldn't name, but it reminded her of home, soft blankets, and her mother.

8

———————

Jasmine sat at the base of the beacon tower with Cally while Bishop climbed. Cally walked around the tower with the shotgun but watched Jasmine more than the shadows.

They hadn't said much in the last few hours. Really, Cally was the only one talking. Jasmine didn't much feel like speaking, and Bishop had only said a few words—nothing at all to Jasmine. When they came to the tower, Bishop just parked and said "Stay sharp, Cally," then started climbing.

No discussion, not a single look at Jasmine. There was no need. Jasmine would have done the same. In her mind, she went over and over the day's events and couldn't understand why she had acted like that. She had always thought that when push came to shove, she could do what needed to be done. The truth: when it really counted, she was a coward.

She sat on the ground, looking up at the tower. "Shouldn't be surprised, Jas," she said staring at the winking red light. "Not like you've ever faced anything in life. Always running, always the coward. It's a wonder you didn't get more people killed while you were alive."

Cally turned the corner in her patrol and started walking toward Jasmine. The woman had held her for about an hour, rocking and humming tunes to her until Jasmine murmured a thanks and crawled into the back seat. She laid down with a blanket over her and shut her eyes. A few minutes in, she realized she didn't have her seatbelt on and wondered why Bishop hadn't yelled at her. Given his treatment later, she supposed he didn't much care if she survived a crash.

The night before, when they thought Jasmine asleep, Bishop had said something she couldn't make out. Cally replied it wasn't Jasmine's fault. Bishop muttered something to which Cally said "him neither." Deader fingers reached for her each time she started drifting to sleep. It felt like she hadn't slept at all, but she had dreamed.

In her empty house, in an empty bedroom, she folded her clothes neat and removed the laces from her boots before arranging them neat as a store display at the edge of her sheets. She turned to the white box and pulled at its golden ribbon, removing a vial, a spoon, and syringe. The vial's contents bubbled in the spoon over a candle while she sang to herself. A tiny bite inside her elbow and she flopped back. It wasn't like she wanted to kill herself she just didn't care if she lived anymore. The world turned white, her body sang. What a perfect birthday. A spot before her turned dark. An angel whispered things into her ears she couldn't understand. Jasmine shook her head from side to side, falling now.

"It's not my fault," she said. Then her chest exploded.

Jasmine rubbed at the spot on her elbow where she remembered sticking the needle. Cally walked by and gave her a smile as she passed. Jasmine smiled back, weakly. For all the things she was mad at the real-world Kelly for, leading her brother on, the act at his funeral, this Cally didn't deserve her anger. The woman wasn't even really Kelly, Jasmine thought. Cally was someone else. All Jasmine had done since meeting her was treat her like crap. And she had treated Bishop even worse.

He could have just left her, or killed her, or left her to the deaders. Why he was up there on the tower with a bum hand still helping her find her dead brother she didn't know. In his position, she would have left herself on the road long ago. A useless girl who couldn't fight, couldn't help, or even survive on her own for single night. Her only party tricks were bringing dead plants to life by bleeding on them and making deaders talk. In the grand scheme, not even as useful as a can of lima beans.

Maybe she should just make it easier on everyone. Cally passed her and gave her another smile. It was too much to take, the pity from Cally and the anger from Bishop. She didn't even belong here, in this hell her brother had made. She made up her mind.

She waited until Cally was at the farthest point away in her circuit. Jasmine got up and went to the ladder. Her Keds climbed the rungs quickly and quietly. She was ten feet off the ground before Cally shouted her name.

Jasmine took the rungs as fast as she could, each rung a bit closer to her goal. She glanced down and saw Cally nearly at the bottom rung, shouting at her. She looked kinda funny, Jasmine thought, her mouth made a dark O that perfectly matched the dark circles around her eyes. She looked like a kid's drawing. With the added shadow of her cleavage, it almost looked like one of those emoticons her friends always insisted on putting into their emails. She looked back up the ladder with a smile on her face, how would one go making that on the keyboard? Three rungs later, she had it: colon and a sideways exclamation point. Five rungs later, she realized that wouldn't work. Oh well, it wasn't that important anyway.

The ladder vibrated under her, Cally must be climbing up to catch her. She focused on the rung above her.

"Just a bit farther," Jasmine said.

She heard gasping beneath her. She looked down and saw Cally frozen on the ladder, looking down at the ground. Jasmine had forgotten about Cally's fear of heights. Even better.

Thirty feet, forty, the rungs passed beneath her hands as she calmed her mind. Her breathing slowed in time to the red light and darkness. She stopped when it felt right. She looked down and decided she was about two-thirds of the way up. Where to land? Somewhere away from the car and Cally, preferably near something that would benefit from her blood splatter. She picked a point with two small smudges that could have been bushes or rocks; why hadn't she thought about this earlier? She should have scouted ahead of time.

She turned herself around on the ladder and stood with her heels on the rungs, arms above her head. She closed her eyes and let the red light play over her eyelids. Breathe in—red light, breathe out—darkness. Jump a little bit away from the ladder so you don't bounce on the way down. The ladder is thrumming, but don't panic, it's just the wind. Feel it caress your face, you're ready now. Just breathe.

And jump!

But her body didn't move. Her hands didn't respond; her feet were glued to the rungs. She felt her heartbeat quicken as she felt her will to jump draining. The vibrations in the ladder were getting stronger, making her hands grip that much tighter. No, she thought, let go, who cares? But her weak half, the coward that had made her run earlier today wouldn't let go.

"Settle down, Jas, just do this," she said. "It's so damn easy. Let's go. Jump!"

Her knees bent and she leaned forward, but her body still felt fear clenching her chest and freezing her limbs. A cold tendril crept up her spine, reaching for her brain. If it got there, she knew she would lose her nerve.

"Now or never, Jasmine. No more pain. No more nothing." She filled her lungs and held a breath.

And—jump!

Her hands released, and she went into free-fall. She jerked short, hanging by one arm. She looked up and saw Bishop's hand on her wrist. His gritted teeth flashed white and red in the beacon's reflected light.

"Grab onto the ladder," he said through his teeth. He was shaking, the veins in his outstretched arm standing out. His hand was slick. She felt her skin slide past his palm, slipping millimeter by millimeter.

"Just let go, Bishop. It's okay."

"No," he said. "Grab on."

"You know you want to, Bishop. Do it. I want you to." She looked at him, memorizing every feature, the curl of his hair, the wide nose, full lips, each hair on his unshaven face. She would take his face with her all the way down and into whatever awaited her afterward.

In his eyes, she could see herself already falling. Her death passed through his head, she knew it. Then something seemed to steel itself within him. With a grunt, he swung her to the ladder, and to her shame, she reached for it and held tight.

"Not now, not ever," he said.

THEY STOPPED by a Curdy's Grocery. Bishop went in alone, supposedly to find supplies, but the cracking wood and shattering glass suggested a tantrum. Jasmine wondered whose face he saw, Ryan's or hers.

She and Cally sat on the Biscayne's hood. The shotgun sat across Cally's lap, and she absently stroked its barrel.

"You don't understand, Jas. Out here there is no more hope than you can watch over with a gun or put a wall around. There are only a few places worth doing that for. You keep your hope hidden or you build a fortress around it, or you snatch it and run like hell. But if you can fix this place, then all that stops."

"I don't think I can fix things. If I bleed on something, it comes back to life. Then what? I can't make it rain. There's not enough blood in me to fix all this."

"You won't need to, all it'll take is a few demonstrations, and people will come together and help. We'll figure out how to keep everything alive."

"More like they'll come together and kill me."

"No one will kill a golden goose."

"Really? And the goose gets to walk around? They'd lock me in a cell and bleed me off as needed."

"At least you'd be safe," Cally said.

"I'd rather die."

"You don't mean that."

"Who knows? Maybe I'll end up in heaven."

"I doubt it," Cally said.

"What do you mean?"

"Nothing."

The front door of the Curdy's slammed open and Bishop shouldered his way past its newly bent frame. He tossed an empty can in the air a few times then spun around and threw it like a discus, screaming as he released. The can sailed into the sun.

"Are the cupboards bare?" Cally said.

"You goddamn well know they are."

"We'll find something later," Cally said.

"Fuck all, we will. There is no we. *We* would fucking imply that we all contribute something. I find the damn food. You cover my ass while I do so. Her, I don't know what the fuck she does for us."

"Back off, Bishop. We've all been there. Everyone panics. Everyone makes mistakes."

"I swore that shit off. I'm through with it." He looked at Jasmine and shook his head as if in disbelief. "And here I am doing it again."

"Sorry, Bishop."

"I've saved your ass how many times, and you want to just throw that away? Think you'll end up somewhere better? Not hardly."

"Who asked you?" Cally said.

"She doesn't think about anyone but herself, Cally. And no further than her next step. Remind you of anyone you know? Someone else who ran away and left you to the deaders? "

Cally gathered a breath, seemingly about to tear into him, but she straightened and gave a saccharine smile.

"Fuck you, Bishop, you know?" she said. Cally walked off, flipping her middle finger at Bishop in passing.

"You really think that about me, Bishop?" Jasmine said.

Bishop pursed his lips as he watched Cally walk away. "I think you're dangerous, Jas. You gotta wake up and look around before you get us all killed."

"Then why not leave me right here? You and Cally can get in the car right now."

"If you were anyone else, I would."

"Don't do me any favors because I'm Ryan's sister."

"Not because of that, because you're the closest thing we have for a chance of making it through this fuck-up your brother made."

"If I don't kill you first."

A small smile. "If you don't kill us all first."

"I'm done with suicide," Jasmine said.

"I wish I could believe you."

"Me too."

They spent the next few minutes watching Cally stalk the perimeter, her head bobbing like she was talking to herself.

"I don't get why she's here," Jasmine said.

"Why's that?" Bishop said.

"The girl Ryan pined over wouldn't last a day out here."

"You're the expert now, aren't you?"

Jasmine punched him in the arm. "Listen to me."

He smiled. "Okay."

"Kelly came to Ryan's funeral a wreck. She looked like she had cried all night. Someone must have told her he had a crush on her, so she had some kind of guilt trip going on and the other skanks ate it up. They flocked to her and hugged her and cried alongside her like she was the victim."

"Wasn't she? Maybe she did like him but didn't see the signs."

Jasmine glared at him, her eyes welled up. Funny that it still hurt so much. "Kelly was clueless. She was incapable of noticing anything besides herself. That's what I mean about Cally. She's wiser somehow. She's as much a part of this place as the rocks and dust."

"She's had time to learn, Jas. Lifetimes to learn."

"She's no older than me."

"You'd be surprised."

"How old is she?"

He paused, searching for the words. "It's not how old she is, it's how many lives she's had to live it."

"You lost me."

His hands combed through his hair, tugging and twisting at the ends. "Let's just say there have been many Callys, and each one has come to a bad end."

Jasmine thought about it for a moment. "So this one is a clone or something?"

"More like an improved version of the last few."

"Few?" She lowered her voice. "How many of her have there been?"

Bishop swallowed. "This is the third Cally I've known."

"Does Cally know?"

"No," he said with vehemence.

"You sound certain."

"I would know if she remembered anything from her past."

The way he said it, without the usual layer of bullshit and I'm-too-cool-for-this attitude, made him sound like a real person. Why was that, she wondered. Then she had it.

"You had a thing for her, didn't you?"

Bishop glanced at her with a frown. He let out a slow breath before answering.

"I had a thing for someone who looked like Cally looks, talked like she talks, moved like she moves, all the things our Cally is today. She had a thing for me too. We fought it, then hid it when that didn't work."

"What happened?"

He stared at her.

"Your brother found out. She died."

She stared back at him. A normal person would feel her heart ripping itself in two, but she just nodded, as if this made perfect sense.

"He called her over one day while he was talking to me," Bishop said. "He looked at her like some dog that had crapped in the house. She was talking, then just collapsed, dead before she hit the ground. It was like someone had thrown a switch."

"Bishop–"

Bishop continued as if he hadn't heard her. "I thought he was going to do me too. I could see it in his eyes, that same look the Blood Weeper has all the time. He knew all about us, and I could feel the anger off him like heat from the pavement. Then he laughed and pointed at me, doubled over, said my face was the funniest thing ever. 'Don't worry, Bishop, fourth time's the charm!' he said. He slapped me on the shoulder and walked away.

"The shitty thing is, I don't know if he was talking about her or me. I wonder at night if there are other versions of me out there in the hills or stumbling around deader-style. Maybe one day I'll meet an old me and he'll blow my head off. Or maybe your brother will reach out and flick off my switch because he's figured out what's wrong with me and has a fix."

Jasmine reached out and put her hand into his, a palm rough and gritty with red dust. He gave her hand a squeeze and then withdrew.

"Anyway, we left her there that afternoon as the camp moved on. When we got to the next party, there she was, our new Cally. Your brother puts her arm around her and they go on like nothing's happened."

"Did you ever try talking to her about it? See if she still loves you?"

"Just to see her die again when your brother finds out? Fuck no, I ain't going through that again. Besides, there's something in this new one that is different. Not enough of my Cally made it through. Like hearing someone else play your favorite guitar lick. Does that make sense?"

"There was something lost in translation."

"Yeah, that's it."

"I'm sorry, Bishop."

He shrugged. "If I was running around with her now, I might not have been around for your first date with the deaders. Good thing, huh?"

"Yeah. Thanks."

"Just don't tell her, okay?" He chucked his chin in Cally's direction. "They take the news badly."

When they stopped for the night, Cally informed Bishop he could kiss her ass if he thought she was taking the late watch. She grabbed his rifle and went off to pace the perimeter. Bishop shrugged and grabbed his guitar. He strummed out the chord changes while humming and singing under his breath. Every so often, his fingers would strike the soundboard with a loud drum-like *tonk*.

Jasmine wasn't a fan of the song, whatever it was. Too 80s, too light, probably with lyrics overly concerned with finding the next euphemism for fucking. And yet, as she watched him run through the song, he was somehow able to keep the lyrics, two guitar lines (a lead and occasional rhythm lick), and drum echoes going all while sitting on the Biscayne's hood looking for all the world like he was just taking in the scenery and absently fooling around.

Then Bishop yawned, and she realized he *was* just fooling around. His body moved and swayed like a breeze, but when she watched his eyes, they were far away like someone lost in thought. Distracted as he was, he was still better than anyone she had seen. She bought outrageously-priced tickets to music halls and concerts, having to forego restaurant meals and impulse buying for weeks afterward, and thought it worth every penny to see the top performers in the world. Masters, virtuosos, prodigies, living legends, and one undisputed genius. She wasn't an expert, but she knew talent and craftsmanship when she heard it. Bishop could have played rings around them all.

His song ended, and he stretched like a cat. Then he launched into a new song, a sappy-happy tune from a one-hit wonder. Jasmine shook her head. His playing was effortless, his fingers dancing happily across the frets, but it was like watching Leonardo daVinci painting a fence or Frank Lloyd Wright designing a pole shed. All that talent, consigned to hell.

"Stop it," she said.

Bishop turned to her, playing the same refrain over and over again on the guitar.

"Stop what?"

"Those songs."

Bishop grinned and stopped the endless loop.

"You're amazing—"

"It's what all the ladies tell me,"

"No, I mean your playing. Back in the real world, you could play Carnegie Hall."

"Is that good?"

"It's damn good. I loved going there and hearing the best in the world play."

"So what would you like to hear, babe?"

"I'm not babe. You're playing all this 80s crap, Bishop. Can't you play anything else? Jazz? Bluegrass? Classical?"

"Never heard of any of those."

"Where did you learn those songs you play?"

"I just play what I hear."

"And where do you hear them?"

"On the radio, where else am I going to hear music?"

Jasmine didn't know what to say. It seemed like such a little thing, compared to the Badlands with its famine, deaders, and refugees, but it broke her heart to know her brother had caused this too.

"I'm sorry, Bishop," she said, "that you don't know anything better to play."

"You know better things to play? New things?" He perked up, almost getting off the Biscayne's bumper.

"Sure, there's Beethoven, Mozart, Bach, tons really."

"Okay, hum a bit of one of them and I'll give it a try." He leaned in close, cocked his head, and closed his eyes.

Jasmine shut her eyes and tried to think of a song. Nothing came. She recalled the emotions of all the performances, the music raising the hair on her arms, but she couldn't remember the melodies. She remembered the music, but not the notes. She felt tears welling but held them in check.

"Damn it, I can't." She ground her palms into her temples. "I hate this place."

Bishop stared at the ground for several moments before reaching out and squeezing her shoulder. She should have slapped him but instead relaxed, stepped forward, and leaned her head on his shoulder.

"I hate this place," she said.

"I know, Jas. I know." He placed a hand on her back, and it didn't feel all that bad. She broke away from him.

"Sorry, it's not your fault," she said.

"If you remember a song, just let me know. I can usually get it in the first couple of tries, okay?"

"Okay, I will," she said, but knew she would never remember.

JASMINE DIDN'T KNOW WHY, but when Bishop later offered to take her on a hike, she said yes. She followed him on a path only he could divine, inexplicably turning left or right at landmarks that looked all the same to her.

"What I mean," he was saying, "is that it's a helluva lot better in some ways now that he's gone."

"Ryan, you mean," she said.

"Yeah, your brother. People had to start thinking for themselves, you know? Had to start planning more than a day ahead. "

"Maybe you all were more Zen and living in the moment."

"Nah, that wasn't it at all. People get used to the easy life real quick, and then start freaking out over the littlest things. Maybe your beer isn't as cold as it was last night, but instead of getting up and grabbing a bag of ice, you start bitching to the Man about it. And you know what? He fixes it, on the spot."

"Ryan liked to help people," she said.

Bishop picked up a flat stone and whipped it sidelong, raising a puff of dust some yards away.

"Yeah, and for the next week, he'd remember to fix it so the beer'd be cold and tasty. Then some other pissing and moaning would happen and he'd have to fix that, then the one after that, and so on. Then one day, the beer isn't ice-cold again, and the ungrateful bastards are all 'why are the beers all piss-warm again? I thought you fixed it!'"

"Did everyone complain?"

"No, but enough did. And where are they now? Most are deaders, or getting close to it." He gave a sour smile. "I hope there's just enough left in their heads to realize how fucking good they had it, and how even a piss-warm beer would taste good these days."

"You sure know how to show a girl a good time," Jasmine said.

Bishop scrambled up a rock incline and held out his hand, gritty with dust. "Come on, just a bit farther."

She reached out and let him pull her up onto the rock. For a skinny guy, his grip was strong.

They reached the crest, and Jasmine gasped.

Below them, thousands of hoodoos lined a crater. Each hoodoo angled toward the center like the petals of a thistle or cone flower, or like supplicants bowing toward an altar. The altar in this case being a structure of crumbling metal framework and sun-bleached floorboards. Spotlights with broken colored lenses hung from rusting scaffolding. Behind that, the tattered remnants of a hundred-foot projection screen fluttered in the wind. Dust-covered amplifiers lay scattered like children's blocks with their wiring exposed or innards removed altogether.

"This is the Cradle," Bishop said. "Every so often, the whole damn Badlands would come here and rock. Hundreds of us would be out there in front of the stage, up on the rocks, or wherever. Three days of dancing, drinking, smoking, and fornicating while the band played on."

"Must have been a sight."

He sat on a rock and patted a spot next to him. She sat.

"Your brother would set up there," Bishop said, pointing to a splintered lumber heap. "He had a platform set up in the sweet spot, where the acoustics were best. He'd sit up there the whole time like a kid in a tree house, where everyone could see him. He danced the hardest, whistled the loudest, and drank the most out of all of us. He was like some kind of shaman, leading us to church by example. The party wasn't over until he said it was."

"What was your job, altar boy?"

Bishop laughed. "Hardly. When I wasn't up there partying with your brother, I was there," he said, pointing to the stage, "I'd pull lead on any song that came up and play the shit out of it. I'd start in the morning and just play until I'd realize that it was dark again."

"The band never took breaks?"

"Nah. You wanted to hear a song, you shouted it up to the guys on stage or got a bunch of friends together and played it. I played with just about everyone on stage, taking a break if someone had a hard-on to pull lead on a tune. Everyone in the Badlands knew how to play a couple of instruments or sing."

"Badlands born, Badlands blessed?"

Bishop smiled at her. He had a nice smile. "Yeah, you got it."

"Do you miss it?"

"All the damn time."

She wondered if she should reach out to him or find something to say that would make it better. Nothing came to mind and so they stood there for a few minutes in silence before Bishop let out a sigh and stood.

"Time to head back, Jas."

"Maybe we could come back later. You could bring your guitar and play something."

"Nah, this place is meant for full-power amps. Screaming vocals, wailing guitars, and booming drums. It needs lights, pyro, and a thousand screaming maniacs to live. It's better to leave it alone. If you can't play it like that, it's not worth trying."

When they got back to camp, Cally was cleaning the shotgun.

"So," she said in a lilting voice, "how was your date?"

"It wasn't a date," Bishop said.

"He showed me the Cradle."

Cally leered. "I'll bet."

"Whatever you wanna believe, babe," Bishop said.

"We just took a hike," Jasmine said, "nothing else."

"How could you not fool around? That place always turned me on. Going up there and not messing around is like sacrilege or something."

"Maybe I'm losing my religion," Jasmine said.

"Well it's about time you lost something with him, eh?"

Jasmine glanced at Bishop, who winked.

"Not happening," she said to him.

Bishop shrugged. "If you say so."

"It's not."

"I believe you."

"Good."

As she walked back to the Biscayne, she tried loosening her shoulders to keep herself from thinking about how Bishop's hands would feel on her skin.

9

____

Jasmine and Bishop moved through another picked-over Curdy's supermarket, sifting through the piles of empty cans and looking under overturned shelves for food caches others may have left behind. Jasmine came across a box of macaroni under a dusty freezer case.

"What about this?" she asked, shaking the box to get Bishop's attention.

Bishop glanced and shook his head. "If it ever got wet, it got moldy. No one wants hot bowl of bacterial infection."

"I guess not."

Bishop grinned. "Don't sweat it, Jas, it's not like we're missing out on a gourmet delight."

Jasmine laughed and set the box down. "It would be nice though. I always had a thing for fake cheese on noodles."

"I'd kill for a nice cheeseburger."

"Sausage pizza."

"Cherry ice cream."

"Barbecue," Jasmine said, then remembered the smell of burning flesh at the Love Shack. "Or maybe not."

Bishop peered at the ceiling and squinted.

"Something?" Jasmine said.

"Maybe. Hold this shelf steady, and I'll go up to take a look."

Jasmine braced herself against the shelves as Bishop scrambled up. For a skinny guy, he sure got heavy quickly. Her arms ached as she tried holding the rickety metal steady. She took a peek to see what was taking so long just as a shower of dust tumbled in her face.

"Dammit, hurry up. I'm getting tired."

"The ladies are always saying that to me," he said.

"Do they dump you on your ass too? Because it seems like a good idea right now."

"No need," Bishop said and dropped lightly to the floor with a sack in hand. "Someone left a cache up here, dumb bastard." He began rummaging around.

"Anything good?"

"Madam, tonight we feast on a rare delicacy: Chef Boyardee." He held out a can with a pristine label.

"Dinosaur shapes, nice."

"Nothing but the finest for my favorite girl."

"Oh, so I'm your favorite? Is this supposed to make me go all a-quiver?"

"It happens."

"I doubt it."

"You know, it wouldn't kill you to stop busting my balls every chance you get and loosen up a bit."

"I thought you said I had to be tough."

"Now I'm saying it would be nice to have a dinner without all the moodiness, frost, and attitude."

"Sorry, no can do."

"Really? Even for dinosaurs?" He inclined his head and wiggled the can.

Damn if it didn't sound good though. If he had wanted to do anything to her, or leave her, he would have already done it. Canned pasta as a peace offering? Why not? She let herself relax.

"What the hell," she said, "let's go have us some dinos, cowboy."

"Righteous. Let's go tell Cally what we found. She'll flip."

Jasmine arched her eyebrows. "I thought I was your favorite, and you're already talking about other women?"

Bishop nodded. "Sorry, babe. But tell you what, I'll make sure you get the first helping." He extended an elbow to her.

She took it. "Well, as long as I have some privileges. Let's go."

～

On the way to the next beacon, Bishop's head swiveled to something lying on the shoulder. He turned the Biscayne around, drove a few miles, and parked behind a hill. Cally gave him an odd look and arched an eyebrow. Bishop nodded.

"Hang out here for a while, ladies. I gotta go check something out." He grabbed his rifle and scampered up the hill.

"What did he see?" Jasmine said.

"Bones," Cally said.

"What kind of bones?"

"Bad bones. Ask Bishop when he gets back."

Jasmine tried to get more from Cally, but she got out of the car and told Jasmine to stay put. Bishop returned much later.

"Settlers," he said.

"Fantastic," said Cally.

"You going to tell me what's going on?" Jasmine said.

"Better if she sees it herself," Cally said.

Bishop nodded and opened Jasmine's door. "C'mon, babe, let's go for a hike. I got something I wanna show you." He held out a hand.

Jasmine grasped it and rolled her eyes. "How can a girl resist an offer like that?"

Bishop led Jasmine through the scrub and deadfalls to a hilltop over-looking an encampment.

"What is that?"

"Settlers. Stay down, don't let them see you."

The camp would have fit on a football field and held over a hundred people. The settlers had built their dwellings in a large two-story square with windows on the interior and gun ports facing out. The walls were made from gray boards ripped from various Curdy's supermarkets, bolstered by freezer cases, fluorescent light ballasts, and metal shelving. Barbed wire jutted out from the walls, and each corner tower mounted a huge crossbow made from the leaf springs of cars.

The people were clothed head to toe in light-colored cloth tinged red by the dust. It was as if each one had wrapped several bed sheets around them-selves and used belts, straps, rags, or rope to hold it all together. Heavy cowls and masks covered their faces from view. Tools and weapons were tucked into straps: hammers, pistols, and more than a few knives. The figures clustered in twos and threes, hands near weapons, sometimes grasping them ready to wield when a new figure approached. Jasmine could pick out some wrapped forms that were obviously men, others that were women, but most were ambiguous.

"How to they get in and out?"

"Underground tunnel," Bishop said. "Easily defended, and they can collapse several tons of dirt on anyone trying to get in if things go badly. The buildings are the fortress, and anyone attacking has to either get in through the walls or through the tunnels."

"Maybe they can help us."

"There's no help in the Badlands."

"You and Cally helped me."

"We're the exception. These guys survive by a simple rule: stranger danger."

"We have to be able to offer them something."

"They see just three of us, they're going to wonder if it's worth taking us. Especially if we look well-fed."

"That makes them suspicious?"

"Yeah, these settler types are very clannish. Tend to be cannibals."

"What?"

"Yeah, they eat anything they can find, scavenged stuff from the stores, the deaders that happen to pass by or ... strangers."

"That's awful."

"Badlands cursed, Jas, but they survive."

"So what do we do about them?"

"We go around."

"What if they find us?"

He clicked his tongue. "We run."

"I don't like this place."

"I don't blame you, neither did your brother."

"But he created it."

"Yeah, ain't that a bitch?"

❧

CALLY HUMMED a song Jasmine associated with Cindy Lauper but couldn't say for sure. She sat on a rock with her tulle skirt arranged away from a thorn-covered bush and filed at a nail with deliberate strokes.

"The damn dust gets all over," she said to Jasmine. "It's a full-time job looking this good."

Cally looked up through her bangs, seemingly challenging Jasmine to say otherwise. Jasmine remembered stories of nail files used as weapons in prisons and thought better of making any smart comments. The moment passed, and Cally smiled, returning to her filing.

"You could do with a bit of upkeep too," Cally said without looking up.

"You could keep your mouth shut."

Cally smiled and held her hand out at arm's length, peering at her handiwork. She then seemed to notice Bishop a few hundred yards out, walking the perimeter with his rifle.

"It may not seem like much, especially out here, but such things are noticed," Cally said.

"I'm not interested in Bishop."

"So you say, but even if I did believe you, shouldn't you at least clean up a bit for yourself? It takes pride to survive out here."

"Then you'll outlive us all."

Cally flipped the file in the air and caught it by the tip. She held it out to Jasmine handle-first.

"Give it a try. It's my turn to walk the line."

Cally picked up the shotgun and left. Jasmine glared at Cally's back, then gave up. It was too hot. There was no reason to bother with her nails, it wasn't like she could follow up with a shower. Before she killed herself, she had gone months without worrying about what she looked like. It was great. She ate whatever she wanted, dressed as comfortably as possible, and didn't have to care about what anyone else thought. Even if she was in a seventeen year-old's skinny body, with little opportunity to binge on junk food, why worry about appearances? With only two friends to care about, what was the point?

A voice from a forgotten corner of her mind seemed to speak. *Friends, Jasmine?*

"Are they really?" she said out loud. She watched as Cally said something to Bishop at the perimeter, making him laugh. She found herself smiling too, wondering what was so funny. And there it was.

"Damn," she said. She looked at the file in her hand and at her red-crusted fingernails. She wasn't going to clean them. Her friends wouldn't care if her fingernails were a little dirty. Still, it wasn't like she had anything better to do, so she took the file and began cleaning.

They traveled slowly that day, avoiding the settler's camp, Bishop easing the Biscayne off-road into side canyons and flat stretches of desert. He hummed a tune as he drove, one hand out the window weaving back and forth like an orchestra conductor. His hand patted, smoothed, and stroked, the ground underneath them flowing like taffy before the Biscayne's wheels. Small boulders rolled to the side or sank into the ground. Ruts smoothed. Canyon walls popped and widened around the Biscayne's frame, sending dust and pebbles to pitter on the roof.

"Why can't—" Jasmine began.

But Cally shushed her and whispered, "Don't spoil his concentration."

"He did this before, when the samurai on the motorcycle chased us."

"Bishop can shape the Badlands by singing to it."

"So why not just sing to the road and make it go around the camp?"

"Ask later. Keep a watch out for scouts."

"If I see one, should I shoot?"

Cally looked at her with pity. "No honey, you let me take the shot. Let's not waste ammo, okay?"

When they took a break, Jasmine sat next to Bishop. He took a long pull from a canteen, and coughed hoarsely.

"Cally says that thing you do with the humming can change the Badlands."

"Badlands blessed, so?" He handed her the canteen.

"So why all this sneaking around? Can't you just make the road go around the camp?"

"Because the road is like a river. You can coax it, you can guide it, you can make small changes, but it's going to go where it wants to."

"But when the samurai was chasing us, you made it go all twisty."

Bishop's answer was cut off by a coughing fit. Jasmine handed him the canteen, and after a short drink, he handed it back with a nod.

"Drink some, you need it."

"What about the road and the samurai?"

"Remember the tape?"

"The ones you never play?"

"Yeah. If I can concentrate, can make bigger changes for short time. The Badlands has a kind of rhythm built into it that even the road has to obey. If I can find the right rhythm for an area, I can do more. It costs, but it can be done."

"What cost?"

He looked back over his shoulder. He eyes seemed to drift over every bump, rut, and rock.

"Other than being dead-ass tired for a few days, I can never use that song again. If I get caught in that area later, I have to hope the Biscayne is faster than whatever's chasing me because I can't change the same area twice. These little changes today are small enough and won't spread far, but I'll never be able to work it again."

"I'm sorry." Why was she always apologizing to him?

"Not your fault. Badlands cursed. I've traveled all over this hell-hole, learning the rhythms. I once knew this land like an old friend. But after I change a part of it, it becomes a stranger. Almost all the Badlands are like that to me now."

"Then why go through all this for me?"

"For us, you mean," Bishop said with a small smile. "Because in the Badlands, sometimes you have to leave friends behind to survive."

THEY STOOD OVER HER, waiting.

Jasmine winced in anticipation of the knife's bite. She ran her finger across the blade and let out a little yelp.

"Crap!"

"Next time, just do it quick," Bishop said. "It won't hurt as much."

"I bet you rip off Band-Aids the same way." Not her, she peeled them slowly in a vain attempt to keep any hairs from pulling. "Just let me concentrate."

She let her blood sprinkle the black lump at her feet. It sat on a red Styrofoam tray, a leathery and wrinkled thing reminding her of a monkey's foot. The label attached to the discarded plastic wrapper proclaimed it had started out as a porterhouse steak. It smelled like feet.

"If this works, I totally want bacon," Cally said.

"Ooh. We should have started with that," Bishop said.

"Shut up, the both of you," Jasmine said.

"Who doesn't like bacon?" Cally said.

Jasmine dripped blood back and forth across the meat. The mummified steak just lay there, absorbing it. What if instead of returning to a steak, it became a whole cow? That ought to surprise Bishop, she thought. It would be good to see him caught off guard again. Of course, the resurrection would be short-lived because they'd have to slaughter it. Was that a sin? She didn't know. Still, better to have a whole cow for her efforts than having to cut herself every time she wanted something to eat. Bacon indeed.

"That's enough, Jas," Bishop said. He grabbed her hand and wrapped a bandage around it.

"How long will it take?" Cally asked.

Jasmine shook her head. "The tree took a few hours, the bush a couple of minutes."

Jasmine stared, waiting. What about hepatitis? She didn't have it, but the others didn't know that. How could the others stand to eat food with her blood in it? Wasn't that a kind of cannibalism? Her stomach twisted, and she decided she wasn't going to eat the steak no matter what. She got up and walked out.

"You okay?" Bishop said.

"I'm going out for some air."

"I'll go with you," he said.

"If you like."

Bishop looked over his shoulder. "Cally?"

"I'm on it." Cally crouched at the edge of the splatter pattern and stared at the steak.

Bishop followed Jasmine outside, automatically scanning for trouble. Jasmine tried looking too but doubted she would see anything before Bishop. But it never hurt to learn, right? She scanned the horizon and pinched her shirt away from her sweaty skin, letting a dry breeze give her a little relief from the heat.

"Better?" Bishop said.

"I'm not going to cut a vein every time someone wants a barbecue," Jasmine said.

"Hey, we're just trying something out here. Call it an experiment."

"I'm not trying this out with an empty beer can either."

Bishop laughed. "If this works maybe you could try it on the building itself. Maybe then, everything inside will turn back to brand-new. If it only took a few drops, we could fix things around here."

"And if it doesn't fix a thing...or if it takes gallons?"

He shrugged. "Then we don't do it."

"Or at least not as often, right?"

"I didn't say that."

"Word will get out. People will start looking for me."

"You'll bring them hope."

"Hope?" Jasmine shook her head and ran her hands through her hair. "I'll be what? A savior? A goddess? A golden goose? It won't matter. They'll keep me locked up."

"I won't let them. Neither will Cally. "

"Then you'll both be killed."

"Ain't happened yet," he said, took a quick look over his shoulder at the grocery store, and lowered his voice. "At least not to me."

She turned to him, finding him stifling a grin. Despite herself, she laughed. "That's horrible."

"Yeah, it is. But you gotta stop thinking about the worst that can happen all the time. You need to have a little hope to keep from going nuts out here."

"What do you hope for?"

"Relief. And I want you to save this place. Be better than your brother."

"I don't want to be a god," she said.

"Would it be so bad? Knowing you're helping people, doing something only you can do? Having them see to your every need?"

She heard something in his voice, something tired, almost desperate.

"I'd just screw things up."

"I'd help you."

"Like you helped Ryan?"

He frowned. "Maybe, but we could do better." He placed a hand on her shoulder and looked into her eyes. "He didn't care about anyone else, Jas. You're not like him."

"That's not what you said the other day."

Bishop kicked at a rock. "Yeah, I did. I was pissed at you and said things I shouldn't have. You're nothing like your brother. Deep down, there's a part of you that won't quit."

"Maybe."

"You could bring so much good back to this place. Would it be so bad to be a goddess?"

She thought about it. She could see a city with herself at the center. Mornings going out with a knife to smear her blood over the dead things in the world. Worshippers at her feet, bringing fruit, breads, wine, like something out of Cleopatra. They would sing songs to her and be happy. Was Bishop right? Would it be so bad?

A shrill whistle brought her to her senses.

"Heads up," Bishop said. He pointed to a ridge.

A line of figures, silhouetted against the sky, stumbled down the slope.

There were thirty or forty deaders, far enough away not to be a threat for a few more minutes. A sound like rustling carried on the wind; they were calling to her already.

"Shit," Bishop said. "I didn't think they'd make it here so quickly."

Her blood called them, she realized. Jasmine saw her little vision of Cleopatra's Egypt swept away on a tide of blood and mummified flesh. She would be locked in a tower with a sea of deaders outside. Jasmine Shaw, Queen of the Dead.

Cally walked out with tears on her face. "It's not working," she said.

Oh thank God, Jasmine thought.

"Then we'd better leave before the party comes to us," Bishop said, tossing his head toward the deaders.

"Fuck me," Cally said.

"Maybe later," Bishop said. "Head for the car."

Jasmine walked to the Biscayne, telling herself she would not run. She would let Cally get in first, just so there'd be no misunderstandings. A shot sent her diving to the ground.

"Bishop!"

He lowered the rifle. "Sorry, I had to do it."

"What?"

"That one with the Duran-Duran t-shirt and the gold chain was Two-Time Tommy."

Cally put a hand to her mouth. "No shit? Poor Tommy."

"You recognized one of them?"

Bishop shrugged. "It happens every so often. Used to know a lot more, of course." He put the rifle to his shoulder and swept it across the deaders. "Tommy Archer. Called himself Two-Time Tommy after some bullshit story about how he once banged twins. He stayed in the Badlands longer than most, swore he'd never leave, though he helped me get others out. Then one day he finally realized it was all a lost cause so he shook my hand and took a motorcycle to Paradise City."

"And you just shot him," Jasmine said.

"Wouldn't have recognized him except for the necklaces and the way he walked. Even as a deader, motherfucker has a pimp roll." He looked at Jasmine. "I expect anyone I know to do the same for me."

"Let's leave," Jasmine said.

Cally put an arm around her. "I know it's disappointing, honey. It would have been nice to have steak."

Jasmine's stomach turned as she thought about the bloody mess back at the store. Food was the furthest thing from her mind, though she knew her body would betray her tonight when they stopped for camp. It always did.

IN THE NIGHT, the beacons played hide and seek. One moment seeming so close, then hiding behind a mesa for several minutes only to emerge farther away. They found three more beacons that night, Bishop making each climb to the top, Cally standing guard with her shotgun. Jasmine sat on the car hood and tried to ignore the part of her mind whispering about how easy it would be to just check out. Try dying again, and see what happens. This isn't what she expected from the afterlife, so why tolerate it?

She hadn't thought about what the afterlife would be like, not really. As a girl, she imagined she would wear a Grecian-style linen dress, looking flawlessly beautiful. She would be brought up to the heavens on the wings of a pristine-white bird with an impossibly slender neck, curved bill, and feathers which curled at the ends like breaking waves. She would be taken to an ivory tower with the wind in her hair and from above she'd survey the lush green gardens and cool blue ponds and fountains.

Instead she was sitting on the hood of a rusty Chevy in tennis clothes soiled with red dust, riding along with what passed for the last two civilized people in the Badlands as she tried not to get eaten by zombies or skewered by a psychopath with a samurai fetish.

"Whatcha thinkin'?" Cally asked. Jasmine told her.

Cally looked thoughtful for a moment. "Well, at least you've got a killer bod."

"Ugh. Whatever."

"No, seriously. I'd love to be tall and not have to worry about crushing a boob every time I roll over in my sleep."

"Does that really happen?"

Cally rolled her eyes and nodded. "Yeah-huh, like all the time. It hurts like a bitch."

A laugh escaped from Jasmine's mouth. "I can imagine. But they do come in handy sometimes, don't they?"

"Oh sure, they're like the world's best accessories. Who needs necklaces when you got these?" She struck a pose and shimmied her hips, which pitched Jasmine forward with more laughter. Cally smiled and then sighed. "Not that there's anyone around to notice anymore."

"Well, there's Bishop."

"Sometimes I think Bishop doesn't notice anything that doesn't have four wheels or six strings."

Bishop came down from the tower, with a worried look on his face.

"What is it?" Cally asked. Her eyes went to the perimeter, searching for targets.

"I've got good news and bad news."

"I'd fuck a camel for some good news," Cally said.

"One hump or two?" Jasmine said.

Bishop blinked, and Cally laughed.

"Bishop, I think you're starting to rub off on her," Cally said.

"There's hope for her yet," Bishop said. "Okay, the good news is we're close to the bridge leading to Paradise City."

"And the bad news?" Jasmine said.

"Near as I can figure it, we'll be heading into more settler territory soon."

"That's not good."

"We'll need to watch the road and the mesas for scouts."

"Can't we go around?" Cally asked.

Bishop shook his head. "Nope, we don't have the fuel. I figure we have about a hundred miles left of juice before the Biscayne runs dry."

"So how far to Paradise City?"

Bishop shrugged. "Hopefully less than a hundred miles."

"So what's the plan?"

"We keep our eyes open, keep a low profile, and hope we're not seen."

"And if the scouts find us?" Jasmine said.

"Long pig for dinner," Cally said. "Sooie!" She poked Bishop with her finger as she yelled. "Sooie, piggy. Soo-sooie! Oh, you're so tough, not an ounce of fat on ya."

Bishop swatted her hand away, smiling. Jasmine found herself covering her mouth with her hand.

Bishop gave her a lopsided grin. "Don't worry. We should be able to keep away from them." He turned to Cally. "Ready to go?"

"Saddle up!" Cally said.

"Got your balls of steel ready?" Bishop asked.

"More like tits of TNT," Cally said. She thrust her chest out with enough force to jiggle. "Boom!"

Bishop laughed and shook his head. "Okay, have it your way. Let's go."

Cally cocked one eyebrow and looked at Jasmine.

"I see what you mean," Jasmine said.

"What?" Bishop said.

"Nothing. Let's go." Jasmine let a small grin cross her face. "Shotgun!"

THEY STOPPED in the afternoon at a pull-out with a view of the road ahead. Jasmine went about setting up camp, such as it was. There would be no fire and just a short trench behind a rock for a bathroom. Cally went to watch the road, and Bishop took out his guitar and quietly strummed a tune with his fingertips. Jasmine sat next to him and watched the bathwater clouds swirl toward a faraway drain.

"So where did the Blood Weeper come from?" Jasmine said.

Bishop put down the guitar and shrugged.

"I don't know. One day this crazy motherfucker on a red motorcycle shows up at a party and starts screaming at people. Pretty soon, a guy tells him to shut up, and Kikuchiyo hits him right in the mouth."

"Did he kill them?"

"Nah, all he did at first was fight. They'd pile on and beat the crap out of him. Then he'd leave."

"I take it that it gets worse."

Bishop nodded. "Eventually, he learns how to fight. He starts punching people out. Instead of needing one or two guys to beat him, it now takes three or four. Then another three or four. Soon he's like Bruce Lee, and no one can take him. That's when someone made a mistake."

"They pulled a weapon?" Jasmine said.

"Right first time. A guy pulls a knife and stabs Kikuchiyo in the shoulder. The samurai just stands there, bleeding. Then he starts crying, except instead of tears, it's blood. The guy that stabbed him is all freaked out, along with everyone else. The samurai stands there, screaming, and then blood starts pouring from his eyes. The guy with the knife runs away, and for a moment, it looks like it's going to end there, but no."

Bishop stopped for a moment, staring into the distance and shaking his head.

"The Blood Weeper walks back to his bike and pulls that damned sword out. Big fucker, ain't it? Yeah, well no one had ever noticed he had it. Maybe it hadn't existed until just then, but one second he's weeping, the next he's back on the bike with that big sword, cutting people down. Sliced clean in half and shit. All but the guy who stuck him."

"He got away?"

"No, he didn't. The samurai caught up to him and slashed across his legs. Cut his hamstrings. Then he dragged him back to the camp behind his cycle and left him in the middle of the bodies. We found him a day later, crawling along the road with his legs dragging behind him like dead meat. Wouldn't say more than a couple of words at a time. Took us a month to get the story out of him in little bits and pieces. Meanwhile, every so often a group would go missing, and we'd later find them hacked up somewhere."

"That's awful."

"That's when the party ended. Between him and the deaders, people started leaving."

"You said you and he had a truce once."

"More of a mutual agreement. I was too fast to catch, and he was too damn tough for me to take out. Stalemate. I don't know, maybe he gets lonely, and he wouldn't have anyone left if he killed me."

"Except Cally."

"Maybe he thought your brother was protecting her."

"He was afraid of Ryan?"

Bishop shrugged, "He never did attack a camp your brother stayed at. Seemed to keep his distance."

"But he did attack Cally at the Love Shack."

"Only because you were there, I think. And because he found a way to organize the deaders to overwhelm her defenses. That's the damn thing about it. He was dangerous enough on his own, but if he's out there organizing? We're all fucked."

Cally came running into the camp.

"You gotta come see this," she said.

They ran to a ridge top where a man lay dead, the back of his head caved in. Jasmine had to look away, once she realized the corpse was no deader. It shouldn't have made a difference, but it did.

"Your handiwork?" Bishop said.

"Couldn't risk the shotgun in case he had friends. But that's not why I got you." She handed him a pair of binoculars.

"Look down there, on the other side, but don't silhouette yourself."

Bishop crawled on his stomach and looked through the binoculars. His body went rigid. Jasmine head him blow out a long breath before sliding backward and standing.

"What is it?" Jasmine asked.

"Kikuchiyo. He's in the settler's camp."

"Then let's go," Jasmine said, "We can run past them while they're trying to fight the samurai off."

"It won't work."

"Why not?"

Bishop handed her the binoculars. "Take a look, but don't let them see you."

Jasmine crawled on her belly like Bishop had. Down in the valley, a crowd outside the gates of an encampment stood around a figure in red, the Blood Weeper. He walked about the circle, waving his arms animatedly. She couldn't make out the words, but the body language was the same as she'd seen on TV and old movies. The Blood Weeper was making a speech, sweeping up his arms as he talked to encompass the crowd, rounding on individuals as he was making a point. He unsheathed his sword and held it aloft, drawing cheers from the crowd. Jasmine pushed herself away.

"He's organizing them, isn't he."

Bishop nodded.

"Then we're fucked," Cally said, kicking the body at her feet.

"Not yet. It means we just have less time than we thought. We may need to gamble more, run faster in the open, and hope no one sees us."

"Then the sooner we're out of here, the better," Cally said. She turned to Jasmine. "Right, Jas?"

Why was she asking her? Jasmine nodded.

"Okay," Bishop said. "We'll wait until dark, then make a run for it. Let's go."

"Shouldn't we hide the body?" Jasmine asked.

"Do you want to dig the hole?"

Jasmine looked at the packed ground and realized it would take hours to dig a hole big enough with a shovel, which she didn't even have.

"No, not really."

"Then let's get some rest. We'll need all we can get."

10

———

Jasmine lay on the Biscayne's hood in the shadow of a red rock cliff. Cally's snoring from the back seat had driven her out—as if she could sleep knowing the Blood Weeper was nearby. Bishop strummed his guitar and tapped his pick against the soundboard. There was something frenetic about his playing, like a movie soundtrack for a man running from *banditos* in the hills.

The arcing clouds swirled clockwise as she listened, heading toward whatever drain in the sky called to them. Maybe that was where heaven had gone, sucked into some far-off drain. She said as much to Bishop when he set the guitar down.

"I don't know. You think there's a heaven out there?"

Jasmine rolled her head from side to side. "What do I know, I just got here, right?" She rolled her head and gave Bishop a smile.

"There are some things you have to believe out here, or what's the point of it all?"

"Mmm. I always wonder what the point is." She let out a bitter laugh. "That's how I got here. Then you found me."

Bishop got up and dusted off his jeans. "Move over," he said, and laid down on the hood next to her.

They stared at the clouds for a while before he spoke again. "You ever see Japan?" he asked.

"No."

"But you believe it exists, right?"

"Lots of people have been there. My great grandparents were born there for Chrissake."

"But you've never seen it, never touched it, smelled it or anything?"

"No."

He glanced at her and then back to the sky. "Sometimes, you just have to take a few things on faith, Jas."

"That kind of stuff doesn't work out for me."

"Maybe you should let it."

"Maybe you should shut the hell up."

Bishop pressed his lips together and looked further up into the sky, perhaps looking for divine intervention. Jasmine didn't think anyone would answer his prayers.

Bishop rolled to his side and leaned over her. His hair fell around his face, and she could barely see his eyes.

"You're a very frustrating girl, you know that?"

"I don't like it when people tell me what to do. You do that a lot."

"I'm just trying to keep you alive."

She raised an eyebrow at him. "Seems like the only way you know how is to order me around."

"Sometimes I don't have time for nice."

"I noticed."

Bishop grunted and rolled off the hood. He walked a ways down the road, shaking his head and muttering to himself. Jasmine saw the tightness in his shoulders and felt guilt creep into her stomach. You're doing it again, Jas.

Jasmine got down and ran after him, calling his name. She broke into the sunlight and caught up to him, turning him around by his shoulders.

"What?" he said.

"Look, I'm sorry. I know you're just trying to help."

"Thanks for noticing."

"Look, I'm not good with people, okay?"

He looked at her a long while, chewing on the inside of his cheek. He looked like he wanted to say something, taking in short bursts of air through flared nostrils. Finally, he blew out a long breath, glanced at the heavens, and relaxed a bit.

"I live in the car," he said, "have for nearly a year. Spend most of the time by myself. You get used to that, you know?"

"Sure."

"You know what to expect when it's just yourself. With you, I don't know anymore."

She nodded. He ran his hands lightly up and down her arms. She didn't flinch or find herself wanting to step away. She leaned forward and put her arms around his shoulders as he folded his arms around her back and waist. They held each other in the blazing afternoon heat as the clouds continued to curl through the sky.

He was thin, too thin really, just sparse muscle and skin stretched over bone. His teeth weren't straight, his hands too rough, hair too long, and just all wrong in too many ways. But right now, in this place, it didn't matter. Jasmine felt good for the first time in a long while.

She turned her face up to his and ran the back of her nails against his neck. He leaned down and held his lips just short of hers, still looking at her with a wary look, like he expected her to bolt. She closed her eyes, and their lips met.

It was a tender, cautious kiss, gone in a moment. She opened her eyes and he was still looking at her like he expected her to run. She drew his mouth to hers and as they kissed again, he let out the breath he had been holding.

Jasmine poured all her fear into the kiss, willing it out of her to be burned up somehow where their lips met. They parted only to meet again with renewed hunger. His hands slipped to her hips, and pulled her closer. She dug her nails into his skin and let out a gasp as he pressed against her.

Hands ran inside shirts, soon finding ways to get the garments off and flung to the ground. His fingertips brushed her collarbone, then shoulders, ribs. She leaned back and his hands cupped over her breasts, squeezing before he brought his hands up and pulled her face to his again. Tongues explored, she let a hand drop to his pants and she stroked at the straining bulge from the outside, eliciting something between a groan and a growl from him. She gave a little hop and wrapped her legs around him. A quarter circle, and she had him pressed at her entrance. His hands cupped underneath her, and they looked into each other's eyes as she rocked against him.

He lowered her to the ground and ran his mouth down her neck. His stubble burned and traced a trail down her chest. She looked down and saw his eyes peering out from under his shaggy hair, hungry. He freed her bra a moment later, and she closed her eyes as his mouth closed over a nipple. Warm, wet sensations mixed with the roughness of his hands and stubble. A quick nip from his teeth left her gasping. Then his mouth began tracing a line down her stomach. His fingers hooked into the waistband of both shorts and panties, ready to pull.

"Jas," he said.

"Yes?" She knew the question, the answer would be yes.

The pulling at her waist stopped. His mouth kissed her inner thigh, just under the cuff of the shorts. She looked down and saw him looking not at her but past her shoulder. His eyes had gone cold.

"Whatever you do, keep looking at me, okay?" He kept kissing at her, but his tone had gone sober. Jasmine tensed and almost looked over her shoulder but stopped as Bishop's hand squeezed the back of her thigh, hard enough to make her wince.

"We got company in the rocks above us."

Fear seeped back into her. She nodded.

"When I say, I need you to kick at me, make it look like we're having a fight so I can go get the rifle. You need to distract them long enough for me to make the shot. Got it?"

Tears welled in her eyes. She wanted to wail about how this wasn't fair, but all she said was, "Got it."

"I'm sorry, Jas."

She gave a tiny nod. "Not your fault."

"Okay ready?" Another nod. "Go."

She kicked at his head, or rather the dirt near his head. She jumped up.

"Goddammit, Bishop!" She aimed a slap at his face. He covered up and hunched down, taking the blow on a forearm. He began backing away. She kicked at him, throwing more force behind it than she intended. Her foot connected with his thigh, and he stumbled. He half hobbled, half ran away from her, toward the car.

She shouted after him, flipped him the bird. She ran her hands through her hair and kicked at his t-shirt, not finding it hard to play the pissed-off woman one little bit. One fucking moment of bliss in this place and fate decides it's time to fuck it all up. Well fuck this place with its fucking cannibal perverts I hope to hell they all turn deader, she thought, so I can run their asses over and feed them to the goony birds. How the fuck would they like that, huh? They messed with the wrong bitch this time.

She looked into the hills and screamed. The scream echoed, and she hoped it made their ears bleed. She saw a flash of light in the hills, a glint of sunlight. Then a shot rang out from behind her, a crack that echoed in the canyon before silence fell.

Jasmine turned to see Bishop squinting through his rifle sight. He lay nestled between a rock and the cliff face, the barrel just poking out in the sunlight.

"Jas, get down," he said.

She fell to her knees and scrambled behind another rock.

"Did you get him?"

"Think so."

Moments later, they heard an engine start, then a high pitched revving. Bishop swore and stood, sweeping the rifle across the hills. Jasmine poked her head out and saw a trail of dust pop up in the rocks above. Bishop fired once more, but the dust trail kept moving. A motorcycle's engine echoed and faded.

"Crap, let's go," Bishop said. He reached down, grabbed at his t-shirt, and began running toward the car. Jasmine searched around for her bra and polo and ran after him, struggling to get the shirt over her head.

Cally was halfway between them and the car, shotgun in hand. She looked dazed and opened her mouth to ask a question but Bishop spun her around by the shoulder and yelled to get in the goddamn car.

Bishop slid over the hood and threw the rifle in the back seat, the guitar followed. A second later, the engine roared to life.

"Let's go, let's go, let's go!"

Jasmine made it just after Cally. She slammed the door and they took off in a cloud of dust.

11

"What the hell, Bishop?" Cally said.

"We make our run now," Bishop said, grimacing as he worked through the stick shift's progression. "A scout got away; soon the Blood Weeper will know where we are. "

"Can't we hide somewhere else?" Jasmine said.

He shook his head. "I know this area, so does he. Any place I can think of hiding, he already knows about. With any luck, we'll make the bridge before he can reach us."

As they descended from the mesa, the road gave way to a great plain. To either side, the scrub brush disappeared, the red rocks shrank to pebbles before becoming buried by whitish sand. To Jasmine, it looked like the road ran straight to the edge of the world, a jagged dark scar running from horizon to horizon.

"What the hell is that?" Cally said, pointing.

Bishop said, "The Barrier Gorge." He grinned. "Keeps all the riff-raff in the Badlands, away from the civilized people."

The Biscayne roared onto the plains, and Jasmine lost sight of the Barrier Gorge. It was eerie, like they were on a river and about to hit the waterfalls.

"Hell," Bishop said.

To their left and right, dusty rooster tails streaked toward them. Jasmine could just make out the riders on motorcycles.

"Not good, Bishop," Cally said.

"We'll make it," he said and stomped on the pedal. "We're faster than they are."

The Biscayne's roar grew, raw and ragged. Jasmine was pushed farther back in her seat, and she tired gauging the point where the dusty white rooster tails and the road would meet. As they came closer, Jasmine focused on the dust-covered riders, none dressed alike. One had a helmet and leather riding suit, another ratty jeans and a cowboy shirt, with sunglasses and a handkerchief around his mouth. One other, riding in front, wore nothing but goggles, a loincloth, and a harness around his chest from which a small rectangular pennant fluttered. Their cycles were a motley collection too, from small dirt bikes to heavy road bikes with huge exhaust pipes on each side, even one rider on a three-wheeled cycle. All riding toward them, converging on each side.

"There," Cally said, pointing ahead. Jasmine saw two white posts sticking into the sky ahead of them. Smaller white spokes fanned out from the posts toward the ground.

"The bridge," Jasmine said.

"We're gonna make it," Cally said, pressing forward in her seat. The cycles were closing quickly, just ahead. Jasmine glanced at Bishop. He scanned the road, locking onto the biker with the pennant.

"Bishop?" Jasmine said. Bishop didn't look at her, didn't say a word, just brought the corner of his mouth up in a wicked little grin.

The lead biker mounted the gravel shoulder as they passed. For a moment, Jasmine could see the arrow-shaped tattoo running down his bald forehead, the dust covering his dark goggles, white teeth and a dirty face contorted in rage. His frustrated scream faded behind them.

"Hot damn!" Cally said. "Bishop, you are my own personal Jesus, you know that?"

"We're not out yet. But we should be able to lose them after the bridge."

They roared down the highway. Jasmine looked behind her and saw the cycles were falling behind.

"Shit," Bishop said.

Jasmine turned and her stomach twisted. Ahead, three burned-out school buses blocked the remains of a bridge. Large wooden Xs has been placed in front of the wrecks, about ten feet high. On each X hung a withered spread-eagled husk that had once been human. Heads without eyes jerked up and turned at their approach. The bridge beyond continued for perhaps a hundred feet before ending in crumbled pavement and twisted rebar. The bridge's far side seemed tiny and almost invisible in the haze.

Bishop slammed on the brakes, and the Biscayne fishtailed and screeched. Bishop turned the wheel over, and Jasmine crashed into the door as the car slid around. It came to a stop, facing the oncoming motorcycles at a slight angle.

"What are we doing?"

"Plan B."

"And what's plan B?"

"I'll tell you when I figure it out," he said. "Rifle."

Jasmine passed the rifle over to him, and he stuck it out the window at the approaching cycles. They peeled off the road to each side and came to a stop. As the dust settled, another motorcycle cut through the cloud like a scalpel. The rider rode with a kind of arrogance, in a mottled and ribbed suit of armor that Jasmine hadn't seen outside of the movies or a museum. It would have marked its rider even without the distinctive sword hilt peeking over his shoulder.

The Blood Weeper came to a stop and removed his helmet, scowling at them from behind his scraggly beard and thick eyebrows. He leaned his bike to the side and spat on the pavement. When he sat up, he seemed to be looking directly at Jasmine.

The Blood Weeper shouted at them in Japanese. As the spoke, his fingers pointed at them and then he spread his arms to include his men around him. His speech ended with a clenched fist. Jasmine couldn't make out what the man had said, but she had heard "Bishop" several times.

"What did he say?" she asked.

Bishop reached down and fished under his seat, coming back up with a pair of black fingerless gloves with leather palms. "He said if I give you two over, he'll let me keep the car. Otherwise, he's going to send in his boys." He put his right hand in a glove and brought it up to his mouth, using his teeth to pull it tight.

"What are you going to tell him?"

"He's going to tell them hell no and get us the fuck out of here, right?" Cally said.

Bishop grabbed the rifle with his right hand while he repeated the glove-in-teeth maneuver with his left. "A variation on that," he said. He leaned out of the window.

"Kikuchiyo," he said, "You blew the bridge. Are you getting too slow? You now need deaders and honorless cannibals to do your fighting for you? You are a shameful excuse for a warrior." Bishop gave a toothy smile, then bit at the air between them. "You are already beaten."

The samurai's head snapped back as he let out a guttural roar, which sent tendrils of fear racing through Jasmine's limbs. His sword unsheathed so fast, it was like it had just appeared in his hand, flashing in the sun, nearly blinding her. The samurai leveled the sword at them and shouted at his men. Engines revved like the growls of hungry dogs.

"Bishop, I think we should get out of here," Cally said.

"Wait for it," Bishop said. He leaned into the rifle and brought the barrel up.

The Blood Weeper swept his sword around his head. As he opened his mouth, Bishop fired. The man to the Weeper's right went down, clutching his throat. Bishop slammed on the gas, and the Biscayne roared as it leapt forward. The Blood Weeper and his men rushed to meet them. Jasmine saw the chains, hooks, and pistols they intended to use. Bishop drove straight at them, his lips pressed tightly together.

She was scared yet detached. It seemed unreal to her, in this place where everything had always been unreal. She could see the line of metal coming towards them, hear the engines whine, the war cries, but it was as if it was happening to someone else. She looked at Bishop once more and wondered if he felt the same way. She would ask him when this was all over.

The Blood Weeper caught her gaze with his own hate-filled stare. His bike cut through the dust, his eyes narrowed and sword swinging. Bishop twitched the steering wheel at the last moment, and the Weeper's blade flashed past her, cutting at eye level. Then he was gone, but the sword tip's image stayed in her mind.

Bishop slowed, taking the Biscayne off the road and onto the plain. The bouncing and jostling shook Jasmine from her daze. In the back seat, Cally started rummaging through boxes.

The Biscayne kicked up a huge dust cloud, but darker shapes were moving through and gaining. "I thought you said they couldn't catch us," Jasmine said.

"On pavement, no. But here on the flats, some of them will be faster."

"Then why—"

"Little faith, Jas. One door closes, another one opens. You just gotta know where to look for it." He reached blindly, running his fingers down the rack of cassette tapes and counting under his breath. The fingers stopped, and he pulled a tape out. He gave it a glance, blew on the ribbon with a quick puff, and put it in the player.

"It also helps if you've prepped a doorway ahead of time," Bishop said.

"You have? Since when?" Jasmine said.

"A few years ago I thought something like this might happen. Wait until we pass the stone gates," he told her, "then push this in." He glanced back at Cally. "Anything gets close, blast 'em."

Cally nodded. "On it."

Bishop looked at the side view mirror. "Here they come."

The first one rode up on the left side, riding a bike with a jagged hole in its headlight. The rider began swinging a chain with a grappling hook.

"Too close," Bishop said and swerved the Biscayne. The rear quarter panel tapped the biker's front wheel and the cycle found itself going sideways. Cycle and rider tumbled to the ground and were lost in the dust cloud.

Two more dark shapes came out of the cloud to either side, the riders leery of coming closer.

"Jas," Bishop said, and she turned around. Ahead, two rock formations rose up like little columns. When she looked closer, she realized they were hand-placed cairns, not natural at all. The pair was spaced about fifty feet apart, each cairn made of three stacked red rocks. As they passed, she reached out and pressed the tape home.

The player clicked, then played the sound of a guitar impersonating a motorcycle shifting through its gears. She saw Bishop's hands stretch on the steering wheel, and his fingers curled back around the wheel from pinky to thumb. The drumbeat kicked in and his shoulders flexed with a little roll. More cairns appeared ahead, spaced at even intervals.

The shotgun boomed in Jasmine's ear and a rider fell. The tang of gunpowder filled her nostrils. Cally racked the shotgun, and a spent shell of red plastic and tarnished brass fell to the floor.

"Your side, Jas!" Cally said. Jasmine looked out her window and saw the other rider aiming a pistol.

The biker fired. Not at her, she realized, but at the car. A bullet hole appeared in the Biscayne's side panel, just ahead of the rear tire. The pistol's recoil had threatened to knock the rider off his ride, and he brought both hands down to his handlebars as he fought for control.

The voice on the tape was screaming about skydiving naked and women from outer space. Jasmine pulled the crossbow to her shoulder and fired. The biker's front tire exploded. He was thrown over the handlebars and landed head first as the dust cloud swallowed him up.

The face etched itself in her memory. She saw his eyes widen, the scowl turning to fear. She made herself look away, fearing it was already too late to forget the face. She watched as the cairns passed by and realized they were in time to the drum beat. She turned to Bishop.

"The cairns?"

"Told you the speedometer's broke," he said. "Got one chance to get out, but only if we're going just the right speed. More coming, look out."

Jasmine looked back and saw more shapes emerging from the cloud. The shadows were getting thicker now. She set the crossbow and loaded another bolt. She would have to make each shot count and hope for a lot of luck.

"Lighter," Cally said.

"Glove box," Bishop said. Jasmine opened it and searched around for a lighter. She found it, a small flip-top Zippo with a skull and crossbones. She passed it back to Cally. The blonde had a brown bottle with a red rag attached to it. She flipped the lighter open and struck a flame in one motion. The rag caught, and she heaved it out the window.

The bottle sailed in the air and came down with a glancing hit on a rider emerging from the dust cloud. It burst with a hollow whoosh and a yellow flame bloomed over the rider. He slapped at his arm, only to find his other hand suddenly coated with flame as well. The fire flowed and engulfed the bike, and it dropped back into the cloud. The last Jasmine saw of bike and rider was a vision like a demon on a flaming horse, with arms wind milling. She heard the screams for a moment longer, a shrieking carrying over the engine noise and wind rush.

"Feel the foo, motherfuckas!" Cally screamed. She launched another bottle, with a flame creeping behind it. It landed on the ground behind them, creating a flaming puddle that sent the bikers scattering. Cally's face had a wild look, all trace of civilization gone, leaving only a mania cultivated by surviving wave after wave of deader assaults. She lit another bottle and casually handed it to Jasmine.

Her hands shook so much, she almost incinerated them all. She screamed in horror as she tossed the thing out the window. The bottle exploded just a bit behind them, and for a moment, she thought some of it may have hit the car, but no smoke appeared and the cycles had veered away, buying them a few more seconds. At least she hoped so.

"Seatbelts," Bishop said. Jasmine looked ahead and saw a dirt mound flanked by rows of cairns. Beyond the mound, the ground gave way to the gorge.

"Oh no," Jasmine said, but she brought the seat belt around and clicked it in. Behind her, Cally did the same thing. Bishop's fingers fanned out and rewrapped the wheel just as the music slowed, the drums thundering out beats that seemed to penetrate straight through her chest. Out of the corner of her eye, something dark moved.

She looked into the side view mirror and saw the naked rider with the pennant. His goggled eyes were hidden, but his face was curled in a sneer. He brought up a pistol and took aim. The front tires hit the earthen ramp, and the gun's muzzle flashed. The rear tire blew out and the Biscayne slewed to the side just as it went airborne.

Jasmine's world turned in a slow circle. She saw the gorge rotate into view outside her window. Hundreds of feet below, a thin green line of water cut through sandstone layers. Then there was nothing but sky outside her window. She turned to the front and the land rose above them, the sky below. They were hurtling toward a rock lip with a nice wide sandy area like a landing strip, with boulders on either side. As the car came right-side up, she knew they wouldn't land straight. The car continued tumbling; her side would hit first.

This is how it ends, Jasmine thought, to the sounds of power chords and screeching metal. Maybe it was her fate, to die so much like Ryan had. It was fitting. She was sorry she hadn't found him. Now at the end, she realized how much it mattered to her, how much she wanted to live, to find Ryan and put her arms around him. To see Bishop's face smiling with her. The thoughts flashed through her mind in an eye blink. The Biscayne rotated through the air and the ground came to meet them. Bishop's hand grasped at the air outside his window and twisted.

The world went white, then black.

12

———

Jasmine woke up staring at the sun. Her head hurt. Cally's face appeared with a smile Jasmine found pretty.

"You okay?" Cally asked. "Feel like anything's broken? Can you move your fingers and toes?"

It was nice to have friends like her, to be so concerned. She wiggled her fingers and toes. "I feel okay, can move everything that is, just a bit of a headache."

"You knocked your head on the dash, but it doesn't look too bad."

"How's Bishop?"

"Oh," Cally said, and looked over her shoulder. "Don't worry about him. You just rest."

Jasmine nodded, then regretted it. The ground spun and little hammers reverberated inside her skull. She lay still until their pounding subsided.

"Is he hurt?"

Cally looked back at her and smiled again. "You let me worry about that. You need to stay put and rest." Cally stood and brushed off her dress. Sand crunched under her feet as she walked away.

In her mind, something screamed at her through the fog. It was so damn hard to think. She felt sleepy. Maybe some rest would do her some good. She brought her hand to her forehead to shield out the sun. Something wet coated the back of her hand. She brought it away and saw a smear of blood.

"Craptastic," she said. She licked her hand, tasting the blood's salt and metal.

The taste cleared the fog. The scream in her mind found a voice. She rolled to her knees, and staggered toward the twisted metal hulk wavering in her vision. Her arms and legs wanted to give out, and she had to concentrate to make them work together. Her first crawling step worked, the second sent her sprawling into sand and rock that seared her skin.

Cally's hands fell on her shoulders. "Stay down, Jasmine. There's nothing you can do."

Jasmine fought Cally's grip; she tried digging nails into the girl's skin and biting at her fingers. Cally stood firm, keeping Jasmine upright as the world spun around her. She puked. Cally held her hair clear.

When the retching stopped, Jasmine took in ragged breaths. "Gotta see him."

"You don't need to see that. He's gone, Jas."

"Can save him." Jasmine gasped. "Blood will fix him."

"He ain't no tree. You don't know what would happen to him even if it did work, which it won't."

"Gotta try," Jasmine said. She spat out the last of the bile.

"You know why Bishop never left the Badlands?"

"He told me. He couldn't stand the idea of Paradise City."

Cally shook her head. "No, Jas, it was because he could never leave. All that road hoodoo in him was tied so closely to the land he could never be apart from it. That was his curse."

"Badlands cursed?"

Cally nodded. "Badlands cursed. He was probably dead before we landed."

The words hit her like a blow to the stomach. "You don't know that." But part of her was already accepting it as truth. Part of her knew. She sagged in Cally's arms. The other woman gently laid her down on the ground.

"I do know. So do you, I think."

"I want to see him, Cally." She felt numb but knew it wouldn't last long. "I need to see him, even if I can't do anything. Help me." She looked into Cally's face.

Cally's face was hardened against her but softened as Jasmine stared back. "Okay," she said, "but if I even think you're going to try something with him, I'm pulling you back. Got it?"

"I know," Jasmine said. Cally lifted Jasmine's arm and placed it around her neck. Jasmine stood with Cally's help and they made their way to the wreck.

The Biscayne had landed on its roof rather than Jasmine's side, to her surprise. The roof was crushed to half its former height and sloped farther down on the driver's side. The furrow in the ground marked where the car had rolled after impact until striking a boulder the size of a dump truck. The Biscayne rested on its wheels, front end wrapped around the boulder, windshield glazed white with spider-web cracks and frame buckled in the middle.

"Its back is broken," Jasmine said.

"It got us here," Cally said.

They came to the passenger side door.

"You sure you want to see him like this? Might be better to remember him as he was."

It sounded like sense to Jasmine. Made perfect sense. But she knew she couldn't walk away without seeing him. "I'm sure."

Cally helped her lean into the car. Jasmine barely recognized it. The dash curled around itself. She saw where her own head had hit, leaving a dark red-on-red stain. The back seat had hardly been touched.

She let her eyes fall on the driver's side at last. Bishop still had his hands on the wheel, which was now pushed into his lap. His chest was crushed between the steering column and the bench seat. His t-shirt had several blood stains that met at the seat below him, where they merged and dyed the Navajo blanket red.

She looked up to his face. Blood ran in little rivulets, matting his hair and stubble, continuing down his cheeks and chin until they flowed over the steering wheel and colored his nails. His brown eyes were open, staring at a point on the passenger side floor. She could almost believe they held a kind of peace in them, a calm understanding of what had happened. But really they were just dead, no more expressive than the deaders walking the wasteland on the gorge's other side.

The tears came to her then, and Cally led her away. They sat a little distance away in the shadow of the rock that was the Biscayne's headstone. They held each other and cried.

~

THEY DECIDED to give Bishop a Viking burial. They couldn't have pried him out of the Biscayne anyway, Jasmine thought. She put his guitar in the seat with him, arranging the fret board's shards more or less in a straight line. She and Cally each took a guitar string. Cally wrapped hers around her wrist like a bracelet, Jasmine just coiled hers in her pocket.

"I couldn't find his glasses," Jasmine said as they stared at the car and Bishop's blanket-covered body within.

Cally rummaged around in her backpack and put something in Jasmine's hand. Jasmine looked down at the gold-rimmed aviators.

"I found them outside. I think you should have them."

Jasmine stared at the car and fingered the guitar string in her pocket. "No, I don't want to see the world like he did. You take them."

Cally didn't say a word, she just folded the sunglasses up and placed them on the car seat next to the smashed guitar. She returned to stand next to Jasmine and the two stood there in silence as the sun began descending in the sky.

Cally said, "You want to do it, or should I?"

Jasmine sighed. "I'll do it."

Cally handed her the skull-and-crossbones lighter and Jasmine walked up to the Biscayne. The last bottle of foo lay on the floor, next to Bishop. She leaned in through the window and put her hand on his head.

"Thanks, Bishop," she said. She expected to feel more, but when she willed herself to cry, it just didn't come. Maybe later there would be more tears, but for now she was just wrung out.

She shimmied back and flipped the lighter open. She had to flick the lighter a few times before it caught. The flame danced before her. In the old Viking tradition, the man's woman would be with him in the funeral boat when it went up. Jasmine thought about crawling in and joining him. She shook her head. How pointless killing herself seemed now.

She lit the rag on the foo bottle and backed away. The interior glowed orange and shadows flickered across the windshield. There was a dry pop and a whooshing of air. The interior flashed yellow, then dense black smoke rolled from the windows.

She stopped next to Cally. The smoke and flame fought each other for a window seat, but soon the fire won out as the seats fully caught. Cally began singing in a clear angel's voice. Jasmine felt the song more so than heard it, the notes raced up and down her body and perfectly matched her mood. A sense of loss, sadness, and promise that somehow she'd carry on, though she didn't feel like it. Funny that an 80s song could touch her like that.

The smoke rose in a black column as the car was slowly consumed. The smell of plastic, rubber, and flesh permeated the area, but they watched until the roof caved in, releasing a billowing mushroom-shaped mass of smoke into the air. When Jasmine looked at the car's interior, nothing left resembled Bishop.

"Let's go," she said.

Cally nodded and turned away from the wreck and the gorge. Jasmine said one more silent goodbye and turned to follow.

~

THE BLACK SMOKE column marked Bishop's grave long after they left the wreck behind them. Jasmine and Cally said little to each other during the day, each almost silent in her own thoughts. There wasn't much salvage from the car. A bit of water, some blankets, and an aid kit. The shotgun and crossbow were out of ammunition, but they hoped to find more along the way.

They found and followed the highway's edge, traveling at night to conserve water, sleeping under whatever cover they could find. Jasmine wondered about deaders and settlers, but Cally just shrugged and said they would either find them or not.

The water ran out after the second day. Paradise or not, the sands were no cooler than on the other side of the Barrier Gorge. As they rested, Jasmine felt the sand work its way into her pores and become a permanent part of her. During the day, she sweated and sniped comments at Cally. At night they shivered together under the blanket.

On the fourth day, they heard a buzzing in the sky. Jasmine stared at the mirage shimmering on the black pavement, telling herself she didn't care what that blonde bitch said, she wasn't getting up anymore.

Something tickled at the edge of her hearing. It became louder and echoed behind her. She rolled out from under the blanket they had draped over a dead bush for shade.

"What is it?" Cally asked.

"Shh."

"Goddamnit, don't shush me, skank."

Jasmine waved her down. "Something's coming."

Cally poked her head out from under the blanket and cocked her head to the side.

The whirring became louder, coming their way.

"I hear it!" Cally said.

"Sounds like an airplane or something."

"It must be them, from Paradise City."

"What if it's not?"

Cally shrugged. "Then we die. Would you rather die in the desert from thirst or a bullet? At least there's a chance to live if they pick us up."

Jasmine kept her mouth shut, as much from fatigue as anything else. She shaded her eyes with her hand and searched the sky.

The whirring grew louder, filling her ears with the sound like a giant dragonfly, somewhere between a deep buzz and a series of clicks. The craft appeared sooner than she expected, and lower in the sky.

It was like a cross between an airplane and a Victorian-themed UFO. Six props buzzed from bat-like ribbed wings made from gold-and-red canvas. The wings attached to a stout bowl-shaped fuselage made from what appeared to be copper. Three figures stood within the bowl, and one lowered something from their face and pointed in Jasmine's direction. The craft banked, and headed toward them. Six golden insect-like legs unfolded from underneath, and its wings pivoted upward as it slowed.

Cally waved and hollered as the craft landed.

"Let me do the talking," Cally said.

"Why?"

"Because you're giving off major bitch vibes."

"Bite me, Cally."

"See what I mean? You want to live or not?"

Jasmine looked away. "Fine."

"Thanks, honey. Be sure to not make any sudden movements."

The figures dressed in the same style as the settlers in the Badlands: desert robes lashed with cords and straps, faces covered by goggles and scarves. But while the settlers had been thin and twitchy, the crew was well-fed and walked with confidence. Perhaps it had something to do with their weapons. Two of the crew pointed heavy rifles while a third alighted from the craft and approached with one hand on a holstered pistol, the other held as if to shake hands.

"You two from that wreck a few days back?" the man with the pistol said.

"Yeah," Cally said. "Who are you?"

"Blake. Salvage operator. That's my crew back there, Juice and Bouncer."

Cally drew herself up and smiled. She also arched her back and thrust her chest out, Jasmine noticed. "I am Cally, that's like Kelly but with an 'a', and this is Jasmine. And boy, are we as glad as fuck to see you! We're trying to get to Paradise City."

"Just the two of you?"

Jasmine wanted to grab the shotgun at Cally's feet but didn't trust Juice or Bouncer's trigger fingers.

"We had one other, but he didn't make it."

Blake nodded. "Need a lift?"

Cally smiled. "Wouldn't mind."

"You armed?"

"A little."

"Well, I would appreciate it if we can all stay on our best behavior."

Cally winked. "I'm always on my best behavior."

Jasmine wondered if she could slap Cally without getting shot. She decided to save it for later.

Blake waved at his crew. "Just gather your things here and get in the 'thopter."

"The what?" Cally asked.

"The 'thoper," Blake said, indicating the craft behind them. "'Ornithopter' if you want to say it the long way 'round, though it's a mouthful if you ask me."

They quickly threw everything into the blanket and tied it up. As they turned to the ornithopter, Blake stepped to the side and waved them past.

"Ladies first," he said.

Jasmine walked toward the craft, fighting the urge to flinch as she looked into the barrel of a rifle.

"Bouncer, open the hatch for the ladies."

Bouncer shouldered his rifle and disappeared behind the wall of the open cockpit. Moments later, part of the fuselage hinged open and a short ladder descended.

Jasmine looked at Cally, who nodded. She climbed into the cockpit, little more than a low bench running around the oval deck, broken up at the front by several levers and dials. Juice and Bouncer stepped back to make room for them all and pointed their weapons so they weren't quite aimed directly at her and Cally.

"Be welcome on our humble 'thopter," Blake said.

"Does that include drinks?" Jasmine asked.

"Juice, offer the ladies some refreshment."

Juice unslung a canteen and held it out to her. Jasmine unscrewed the cap and wrinkled her nose at the metallic odor. The rest of her body had no such problem, and once the water hit her tongue, she began gulping it down. A hand pulled the canteen from her mouth.

"Easy, wouldn't want it to come back up," Blake said. He handed the canteen to Cally, who took two long swallows and reluctantly gave it back to Juice.

"Please sit, ladies. We'll be leaving in a moment," Blake said.

Jasmine sat, and it was as if this sent a signal to the rest of her body to go limp. She hadn't realized how tired she was. Cally flopped next to her and laid her head on Jasmine's shoulder. Blake and his crew began prepping for takeoff, stowing the ladder, firing up the engines, and dumping their belongings into a locker built under the seats.

"Is it far to Paradise City?" Jasmine said.

"A little," Blake said.

Jasmine closed her eyes. Her body felt heavy. Cally's head slumped into her lap.

"When we're back on the airship, put them with the other one," Blake said.

Airship? Was that like a blimp? She couldn't remember. Wait a minute, what was she just thinking about?

"What do you think we'll get for them?" one of the others said.

But Jasmine didn't hear Blake's reply as sleep took her.

13

———

This must be the airship, Jasmine thought when she woke up. What surprised her most was the quiet. It wasn't loud like an airplane, with droning engines and the hissing of recycled air. The airship's engines had a quiet hum more felt than heard, leaving the cell silent but for her breathing and the hollow sounds of footsteps on metal far away. Otherwise, the cell lived up to everything she could have imagined in a medieval dungeon. The room seemed to be made of dark shadows and darker shadows. If there was a bathroom or toilet, the former occupants hadn't bothered to use it. The stench stung her eyes.

"Home sweet home," Cally said.

"I call top bunk," Jasmine said.

"I doubt you'd want to lay down on anything in this place."

"But if there are bunks, I'm getting the top one."

"Suit yourself, honey. You'll be sure to let me know when something drips from the ceiling, okay?"

"As long as you let me know what crawls up from the floor."

"Deal."

"So what's our plan?" Cally said.

"Me? I don't have a plan."

"Well you figure it out, and get a move on."

"I thought you were the expert on how things worked around here."

"Honey, after what just happened, I'm out of the planning business. Your cute-ass brother put all this together somehow, and you're the only other person I know with something close to his ju-ju, so that puts you in charge. If your plan calls for kicking ass, then give me a call."

Jasmine took a few steps and found the room divided in half by metal bars. On the other side, a dark lump lay against the shared wall. She scooted over and put her face up to the bars separating her cell from the other and her nose wrinkled against the stench. It was a man, naked but for a rag tied around his waist. His ashen skin was filthy with shit and piss, which seemed to pool around him as if he had lain there for days without moving.

"Whattya got over there?" Cally said.

"A man. Dead, I think."

"Ew. No wait, he can't be."

"Why not?" Jasmine said.

"'Cause he'd be a deader, wouldn't he?"

"Maybe he's going to turn soon. How long does it take?"

"Fuck if I know. I never saw anyone turn before."

"So what do we do?"

"I don't know, poke him with a stick? Get away from him."

"He could still be alive."

"So fucking what? He'll be dead soon enough. Back away, and stay out of reach."

Cally couldn't see the pathetic state the guy was in. Couldn't see Jasmine that well either, she realized. Jasmine reached out and brushed the man with a fingertip. He gave a short groan.

"Dammit, I told you to get away!" Cally said. She ran over and pulled Jasmine by her arms.

"He's feverish, not dead," Jasmine said.

"Not your problem, Jasmine."

"I can help him."

"It won't be enough. Save up your strength for something that will matter."

"Saving me for a rainy day, Cally? I've got to start somewhere."

"On a guy who's going to die anyway? Some bastard cannibal for all we know? It's too dangerous. You can do better."

"I want to do this, Cally. It's important."

Cally gathered herself, squeezing Jasmine's arms. Jasmine couldn't fight her, not physically. Cally, short as she was, had more than enough strength to hold her back. Jasmine's arms began to ache in the other woman's grip. Cally took in a sharp breath, and Jasmine braced herself for a blow.

Cally let out a sigh and relaxed. "You're as stubborn as your brother," Cally said. "I can't hold you forever, and you'll do it anyway. Go try, but I'm going to pull you back the second he even flinches, you got it?"

"Absolutely, Cally."

Jasmine crawled back over to the man and felt Cally sidle up next to her. Jasmine was sure Cally's hands were already reaching for her, but she put that from her mind. Jasmine let her fingers brush the man on the other side of the bars. His skin burned, slimy and gritty under her touch. She let her fingers rest on his back, and she could feel each rib and trace it back to his knobby spine. A slow, shallow breath labored within him.

"He's still alive, I can feel him breathing."

"What's wrong with him?"

"Can't tell."

"So how are you going to fix him?"

"I'm working on it."

She could prick her finger, but the cell was so dirty she'd likely die from some kind of blood poison; there wasn't any way of washing the grime from her skin either. Then she had it, though it was going to hurt like a motherfucker.

"Hold my hand, Cally."

Jasmine bit down on her tongue and choked back the cry though she couldn't do anything about the tears in her eyes. She squeezed Cally's hand hard enough to make her grunt. Jasmine tasted warm salt and ran the wound across her tooth, milking it for more blood, while grinding Cally's fingers together.

Jasmine spat and smeared the saliva and blood over the man. His breathing quickened, and he began coughing. Jasmine's shoulder screamed in pain as Cally jerked her back. They watched as the man began convulsing. His arms flailed about as his legs began kicking, sliding him along the filth-slicked floor in a slow half-circle. He cried out once, and was still.

"Oh crap, I think I killed him," Jasmine said.

"I don't know honey, I don't know," Cally said. "That's some weird voodoo you've got there."

"But what if I did kill him?"

"He was dead anyway. I just hope he doesn't turn into a deader," Cally said.

Oh shit, she hadn't thought about that. Her stomach dropped.

"At least there's a wall between us," Cally said.

Jasmine wasn't sure how much comfort that would bring her. She'd have nightmares about the bars turning to rust and a naked zombie coming to eat her.

The man pushed himself to his knees and moaned.

"Oh thank God," Jasmine said.

"You still don't know if he's a deader or not."

"I ain't no deader," the man said in a hoarse voice. "Though I feel a far sight away from alive right now."

"Sorry," Cally said. "We didn't know how'd you pull through."

The man rolled over and sat with his back against the wall.

"I thought I was slipping into hell. I'll pull through, I expect. Thank you."

"You're welcome," Jasmine said.

"Yeah, just stay over there if you want to thank us. You really stink."

He laughed once before he grimaced and put a hand to his side. "I'll bet. Though you two ain't so fresh yourselves."

"Fuck you, dead man," Cally said. "It's not like they have showers in this flying dungeon."

"No, no, no. You two got the stench of the Badlands all over you. You're lucky they can't smell you like I can."

"Why, you got a sensitive nose or something?" Cally asked.

The man grinned and all Jasmine could see were red gums and blackened teeth. "It's a trade secret. I was what they used to call a necrosonic engineer."

"Like trains and shit?"

"Nah. I designed and tuned dynamos."

"Still lost me, sport," Cally said.

"Name's Helgo."

"You lost me, Helgo."

"You girls really are from the Badlands ain't ya? Must be, all you cats run is petrochem. Finding that stuff's too damn hard over here—dangerous too. Not enough energy for the trouble. Out here in the real world, we use dynamos."

The real world? Jasmine wanted to laugh. Instead, she said, "If you don't use gas or diesel, what do you use?"

"Deaders."

"Pardon?"

"Deaders, those walking corpses that just keep going and going."

"Don't they kind of kill people?" Cally said.

Helgo laughed, then winced, grabbing his ribs.

"If you let them run amok, sure, they can be a problem. But if you have the knack, and can catch them one at a time, you can calm 'em down."

"And that's what you do as a necro-whatsis?" Cally asked.

"Necrosonic engineer. Yeah. Catch 'em or else maintain them in the dynamos."

"So how'd you end up here?" Jasmine asked.

"We were hunting for deaders just outside the Badlands. Found a few too, enough to pay for the expedition, when we start seeing signs there are other salvage crews in the area, and not the kind you can work around. Normally we'd bug out but the underwriter's chickenshit assessor decides we need a few more deaders.

"They jumped our camp and slaughtered everyone except me, would have done me too until one of them with more than two brain cells to rub together figured out I might be worth something and stopped the beating. Fat lot of good that did. By then I couldn't stand and I was pissing blood. Fucking slavers."

Jasmine's heart sank as Helgo's words confirmed what she feared.

"They told us they were a salvage crew."

"Heh, that they are too. Lots of things out here are valuable. Deaders, scrap iron, cheap labor, and pretty girls. That's why you've got your own cell, by the way. They hate it when the girls have already been poked by the rabble. Big honor to have the first poke of a captured woman. More so if it's a virgin. Either one of you a virgin?"

"Are you kidding?" Cally said. Jasmine shook her head.

"Too bad, virgins get treated better, until they're not—heh."

"That's not funny," Jasmine said.

"No? I suppose not, though I'd rather be a pampered virgin for a while rather than spend a lifetime chained like a dog in an engine room. If you gotta be a slave, might as well be a pampered one."

"I'd rather die," Jasmine said.

"Think that's an escape?" Helgo laughed. "You'll turn deader."

"So?"

"Then you're bound in copper and locked into a cylinder until you're needed for energy. You get out only to get hooked up to the engines. Always hungry, always in the dark."

Jasmine felt the walls close in on her.

"We'll escape," Jasmine said. "Help us."

Helgo blinked. "Do you even know who picked us up? The Caliph."

"The who?"

"The Caliph, as in the head of the Caliphate of the Clouds. We're not escaping from that."

"So what, this place is on a really high mountain?"

He shook his head and grinned with his blackened teeth. "No, lady, not like a mountain at all. You'll see."

THEY SAT IN THE DARK, for hours not talking. Then Helgo looked up.

"Time to get ready."

"What?" Jasmine said.

"Can't you hear? The rotor pitch has changed. We're coming in to dock."

"Maybe we're picking up more..." People? Slaves? Scrap?

"Nah," Helgo said, the pitch is different when an airship lands on the ground. We're docking."

"It's dropped from a high A to a middle-high G-sharp," Cally said.

"Not bad. You'd make a pretty good necro, you know Cally?"

"Everything I do is pretty, or hadn't you noticed?" Cally said.

Helgo cackled. "I'm in love."

"She'll break your heart, Helgo."

"Don't they all?"

The airship came to a stop with a soft bump. Helgo murmured something about amateur piloting and waved Jasmine over.

"There's a debt between us, Jasmine. One that needs repayment."

"No it doesn't."

He reached through the bars and closed his hand around her arm. "When it's in my power, I'll find a way to repay it."

"So I guess you'll have to find a way to free us then, won't you?"

Helgo sighed and let go. "Just one more item on my list of things to do."

AT FIRST, Jasmine thought they had landed on a walled mountaintop compound but then the ground shifted as the wind changed, like a boat caught in an ocean swell and she realized she was on a flying machine as large as a city. As she turned she saw rows of props larger than windmills churning on enormous nacelles, airships bobbing from masts and minarets, and clouds scraping against a dragon-headed prow. The buildings around her reminded Jasmine of a Disney-interpreted mash-up of ancient China, Japan, and the Ottoman Empire. Around the flight deck, arched breezeways led to barracks. Above the barracks, four stories of more breezeways stacked atop each other like building blocks, ending in white adobe walls topped with red tile pagoda-style roofs. Between each archway, demonic *Oni* carvings glared and snarled. Armed men walked with knives and pistols lashed to their desert robes. Women wore similar robes in brighter colors with veils like something from *Arabian Nights*. Behind her, the giant celestial dragon's golden head rose, sunlight reflecting from its emerald eyes. To each side, the massive props blurred over rooftops, generating a low-level thrumming through the soles of her shoes.

She and Cally were kept next to the airship, some distance apart from Helgo as another man approached leading a small squad of guards. He would have been good-looking under other circumstances, with a long oval face, thick Caesar-cut hair, and a cropped beard that didn't hide his boyish face. Dark skinned, he wore an expensive-looking blue suit with a gold tie, which he smoothed as he waited for Blake's report.

"A necro," Blake said, nodding at Helgo, "plus these two."

"Show me their hands."

Jasmine and Cally's arms were forced up. The man looked closely at their hands, and his tongue clucked when he found the split skin and cuts on Jasmine's thumbs. He took a few steps back and looked at them with pursed lips.

The man nodded. "Very well." He turned to his escort. "Take the necro to the power plant and have Jotun find a use for him one way or the other. Take the women to the *hareem* and let Patel inspect them."

Cally spat, sending a glob that landed short of the man in the blue suit. "You fucking kidding me? No way am I going into some kind of harem. I'll bite the balls off anyone who touches me."

The man in the suit looked at the spittle near his toe. "Then it is well that I'm sending you to a eunuch. I would suggest you mind yourself. If Patel doesn't think you'll work out, he'll give you to the guards. When they're done you will either become a house slave or you will power the Caliphate. These are your choices." He leaned forward with an earnest look. "Were I in your position, I would pick the *hareem*. It is an easier life."

"A slave just the same," Jasmine said.

The man in the suit shrugged and then nodded at the guards, who took the women's chains to lead them away. Jasmine turned and caught Helgo's eye. The necro gave her the faintest nod before she was jerked forward and told to face front.

The guards shoved her forward, toward a gate five stories tall leading to a Mandarin palace. Two figures, laughably tiny compared to the gate's arch, stood in red lacquered samurai armor. Jasmine felt a cold stab in her stomach even though she could tell neither was Kikuchiyo. Above them, in the gate's parapets, robed figures paced with rifles. She headed for the palace, only to be jerked sideways toward a small door well away from the main gate.

The dimly lit corridors of rice paper walls and bamboo flooring did little to dampen the props' vibrations. Jasmine quickly lost her sense of direction, pulled this way and that seemingly at random. At one intersection, the guard stumbled over a kneeling woman sanding the floor. She covered her head even before his foot lashed out. Jasmine stared at the cowering woman as they passed. She had been beautiful once, but that beauty had been burned away by starvation and hard use. One of the woman's hands had a puckered scar across the palm. Jasmine met her eyes for a moment and was shocked to see a look of pity on the other woman's face.

They left the maze and came to a larger hallway finished with marble floors, Persian rugs, and statues set in alcoves. The guards jerked Jasmine and Cally aside as courtiers in silk robes and glittering jewelry passed by. Their journey ended at an archway flanked by two heavyset men with pikes. The guards took them to a screened alcove, secured Jasmine and Cally's chains to rings set in the walls, and pulled a nearby rope. Bells tinkled far away. The guards left them.

"What now?" Cally said.

"I don't know. Do you think you could find your way back to the ornithopters?"

Cally looked back over her shoulder. "I don't know, maybe."

"Then we wait and look for a chance to get out."

They were interrupted by the sounds of feet scuffling along the carpet ahead of them. A man with long graying hair and dressed in a blue robe approached them.

"Welcome to his Excellency's *hareem*, young ladies. My name is Patel." He spoke with a high, soft voice. He walked toward Cally and extended a cupped hand to her face.

"Welcome, little flower," he said. Cally's hand flew up to strike him, and then she was on her knees with a silent scream playing over her face. Patel held her arm in his hand with fingers pressing tightly just inside her wrist.

"I am disappointed in you, little flower." He spoke like someone chastising a kitten. "I am here to protect you and see to your needs. But I will not tolerate such behavior from my Caliph's flowers." Cally had managed a thin wail, gasping as her breath gave out.

"Let her go," Jasmine said.

"If I do, will you convince her to behave herself?"

Jasmine nodded. "Yes, yes, just let her go."

Patel released Cally and she snatched her arm back, rubbing her wrist. Patel smiled down on Cally.

"You see? Not even a bruise. Now please don't make me do such things again; I do not enjoy it. Furthermore, your companion has spoken for you, and I should hate to visit the same punishment on her for your actions."

Cally got up and stood still as Patel inspected her. He muttered things under his breath, noting details and flaws alike. Jasmine forced her fear down and stared ahead. As he stood back he nodded.

"Yes, you'll do I think." He clapped his hands twice, and a woman with kohl-lined eyes and a bejeweled veil appeared. Her facial features were a mystery, but she had a chest like a dead heat in a zeppelin race—her primary qualification, Jasmine thought. Her clothing was comprised of diaphanous wraps and loose silks with one leg bared to mid-thigh and a jangling ankle bracelet which tinkled with each step.

"This is Mara, who will guide you around the *hareem* and provide any other instruction you may need."

Mara looked at Jasmine with unfocused, glassy eyes.

"Mara, these are our two new flowers, Dahlia," he pointed to Cally, "and Orchid." He pointed to Jasmine.

"But my name is—" Cally said but stopped as Patel's eyebrows came together.

"All flowers receive a new beginning in the *hareem*, Dahlia." He turned to Mara. "Please take Dahlia and make sure she is inspected. Then you may strike the chains."

Mara turned to Cally and took hold of the chain. She inclined her head and led Cally down the hallway. Cally looked back once at Jasmine, who tried to give her a small nod.

Patel took Jasmine's chain and led her himself. She had always pictured harems as places where ladies lounged on divans around fountains and orange trees. The Caliph's *hareem* was more a large dark room where near-catatonic women wrapped in sheets lay around a hookah set in the middle of a carpeted floor, painted lips drawing in sweet-smelling smoke and blowing it out. The scent masked a fouler permeating smell of stale sweat and urine. There may have been five or six women in the room; it was hard to tell with the haze in the air. Jasmine coughed as Patel led her through.

"Oil of poppy," he said. "One of the many luxuries afforded to the *hareem's* residents."

He led her into a small room with a mattress on the floor and a tiny wardrobe. Patel pulled the curtain closed and had her stand in the room's middle while he lit a small oil lamp on top of the wardrobe.

"Now, Orchid, let us see to you," Patel said. He ran a hand down her face and pulled down her eyelid. He had her open her mouth and looked at her teeth. He loosened her ponytail and shook out her hair. He tilted her head one way, then the other, and muttered things Jasmine couldn't understand.

He grabbed her wrists and looked over her arms, then her hands.

"Bah," he said as he saw the cuts and scrapes. When he flipped her hands over, he muttered some more and rubbed at her dirty fingernails.

"You will bathe and see to this, yes? Then apply cream to the skin. I will not send flowers to the Caliph with rough scullery hands. Now your clothes, remove them."

She hesitated but decided her chances of escaping were better if Patel thought her docile. She slipped the shirt and shorts off and kicked off the Keds. Her face burned as she stared straight ahead.

"The rest," Patel said.

She opened her mouth to protest but was brought to her knees as Patel drove a finger into her solar plexus. Her diaphragm spasmed, and she could not breathe. His hand pinched at her wrist and pain shot through her like electricity. She cried out, and he released her.

She removed her underwear and stood still while Patel poked, prodded, and groped at the ribs, breasts, belly, and buttocks. He continued his muttering like he was having an argument with himself. Jasmine tried to make herself feel numb, like it was happening to someone else, but each touch felt like being smeared with dirt.

She held it together until he pushed her down on the mattress. He brought out a small brass penlight and brought his fingers between her legs. He knelt down and switched the light on. The tears started then.

He stood and put the penlight into his pocket. "You may get dressed from the wardrobe, Orchid. You will be a very special flower." He smiled with a far-off look in his eye. "The Caliph will be so very pleased; it has been a long time since he has had the pleasure of a virgin."

∿

"I DON'T GET IT," Cally said.

Jasmine sat huddled in the tub. The steaming water stung her skin and opened her pores but had not been able to make her feel clean. It was irrational, she told herself. But then again, nothing in this world made sense. She was a harem girl on a floating palace. She was the sister of a god. Her blood could bring things back to life. But she wasn't herself. She wasn't sixteen, she shouldn't be a virgin, she shouldn't be alive. She should have died the first time, or the time after that. She should have died with Bishop.

"I don't know either, Cally," Jasmine said. "I just don't know."

It would be easy to slip beneath the water, a voice whispered in her head. Her forehead dipped toward the surface. She was dirty from the inside out, she thought.

"What do we do?" Cally said. The water in her own tub gurgled as she reached across and touched Jasmine's shoulder.

"We wait for our chance."

14

Cally was summoned on the first night. At least Jasmine thought it was the first night, there were no windows, no clocks to measure time. From what she could see, and based on the sparse, spacey comments from Maya, the women slept when tired, ate when hungry, and passed time as they could at either the hookah or the baths. Jasmine catalogued the *hareem's* contents, trying to find something she and Cally could use when they escaped. For example, she could use the oil lamps like they had the foo bottles, were it not for the watchful eye of Patel, who patrolled every fifteen minutes, making sure everything was in place. Frustrated and worn out, she lay down in her room and closed her eyes.

When Jasmine woke, she couldn't tell if it had been a nap or something longer. She checked Cally's room next door. She wasn't there. A nap then. Cally would have woken her if she were back from the Caliph's chamber. She padded through the *hareem* to the galley and picked at some bread, nuts, and dried fruit sitting out and washed it down with weak wine.

As she passed through the hookah room, a hand grabbed at her ankle. Jasmine looked down into unfocused blue eyes.

"Jaz," Cally said, "howz it goin'?" She rolled to her stomach and took a pull from the hookah pipe. As she did, Jasmine saw fresh red welts raised on Cally's back. Jasmine stood shocked for a second then knocked the pipe away.

"Come on Cally, let's go." She reached down and tried to put the other woman's arm over her neck.

"Leave Dahlia be, Orchid." Patel's high voice said from behind. "The poppy will help the pain until she heals."

Jasmine turned and balled her fist. "What happened to her?"

"She provided the Caliph with most vigorous sport. From what I was told by his majordomo, the cries of pleasure could be heard throughout half the palace."

"She's been beaten," Jasmine said.

"Flowers suffer the elements of life, it is my duty as their gardener to tend to them and make them strong again."

He said it with a sincerity that made Jasmine stare. Patel looked down on Cally with a kind of pity, and he clucked his tongue. "At least the skin is not broken, it will make her recovery that much faster. The Caliph has asked for her again tonight."

"Let me take her to her room, she doesn't need any more poppy."

Patel looked up, mildly surprised. "Are the flowers to teach the gardener his craft now?" He raised his hand. Jasmine braced for an attack, but he just smiled at her flinch. "Very well, Orchid, take your friend to her room. She will need her fire back by the evening."

Jasmine lifted Cally, grunting under the woman's near dead weight. Patel smiled at her as she made her way across the room.

"Orchid?" Patel said as she got to the doorway. Jasmine twisted her head around. "You didn't say 'thank you.'"

A small flame of anger kindled in her mind. "Thank you, Patel."

"You are most welcome, Orchid. Please do not hesitate to ask me for anything that you should need for Dahlia." He gave a little bow and kneeled down among the women.

Cally whispered to her as she led them to the room. "He was wonderful, Jas, handsome, powerful, knew just how to touch me."

"He beat you."

"Mmm. Just got a little over-excited that's all. He said he was sorry afterwards. Promised it wouldn't happen again."

Jasmine reached Cally's room and put her down on the mattress. "Just rest," she said. Cally murmured and settled down. Jasmine brushed at Cally's hair with her fingers.

"Don't like the bodyguard," Cally said. "Angry eyes." Then she seemed to relax, and her breathing became deep and regular.

Jasmine pulled the sheet back and looked closer at Cally's welts. She couldn't tell what had caused them, but they crisscrossed each other, straight lines of raised skin about six inches across. She felt the tiny flame of anger in her burn. She got up and crossed to Cally's wardrobe, sweeping the clothing to one side and looking for something sharp. Unsurprisingly, there was nothing even close to a blade, but she happened to find a pair of earrings with thin posts. She took them across the room and sat down next to Cally. She worked the post across an old cut on her thumb, grinding her teeth as it set her thumb on fire. A droplet of blood appeared, and she pressed it to Cally's mouth.

Within minutes, the welts began disappearing. Jasmine lifted each of Cally's eyes, and the bloodshot vessels had also cleared.

"Rest easy, girl," she said.

She heard Patel's footsteps approach and met his gaze when he poked his head into the room. He merely nodded and continued with his rounds.

The Caliph called Cally seven more times. Each time, Jasmine took her back to her room and tended to whatever welts, scratches, or bite marks she found. Jasmine even risked using her a few drops own blood to seal wounds that would otherwise leave scars. She bathed Cally when she woke up, washing off the dried blood and semen. They ate together, talked, though Cally always seemed somewhere else or stared at the hookah. Jasmine grilled her on the palace layout outside the *hareem*, but Cally didn't have many details to share.

"He is so good. You'll see." She sat in the tub with hot water up to her neck, a towel rolled over her eyes.

"I don't want to see. I want to get out of here. We need to find Ryan and set things right."

Cally shrugged. Jasmine wanted to push Cally's head under the water but reigned in the impulse.

"We can't let Bishop's sacrifice be for nothing," Jasmine said.

Cally brought a pink hand out of the water. Droplets fell from her fingertips onto her face. "They were lovely boys, but do you really think they could have fixed anything?"

"Sounds like you want to stay here, hang it up."

Cally shrugged. "Would it be all that bad? We don't have to do much here. Got hot water," she sank lower in the tub, "food, protection, and a place to sleep."

Jasmine frowned. "It's a cage."

"It's all a cage, honey. Just a matter of how comfortable it is." She lifted the towel and looked at Jasmine. "I've lived in a lot of cages, and this one seems better than most."

"Says the strung-out hooker who gets beaten every day."

"Beats getting eaten."

Jasmine pushed herself from the tub, sending water sloshing all over the floor. She wrapped a towel around herself. "If you want to stay, fine. But I'm getting out of here before some fat bastard gets tired of raping me every night and decides to pass me around or toss me overboard or whatever they do around here with used whores."

"You're such a child. Your kind were the first ones to die, you know, when it all hit the fan."

"My kind? What does that even mean? Come on, Cally, we don't lie down, we fight."

"You mean like you did back in the Badlands?" She laughed. "You talk tough in the bathhouse, but we both know what'd happen out there when shit gets real."

Jasmine stormed out of the room, letting the flame of anger burn a bit brighter. She'd prove Cally wrong. She was a fighter now.

Or at least you'd like to think so, eh Jas? Then why are you crying?

Jasmine was sitting on her mattress when Patel found her. "Orchid, tonight is a glorious one for the Caliph, for tonight he has decided to appreciate the rarest flower." He smiled. "You will make yourself ready within the hour."

"I don't feel like it," Jasmine said.

"This is unfortunate. If the Caliph is displeased, you will be brought in chains and tied down like a she-bitch. The love marks you have been tending on Dahlia will be as nothing by comparison."

She locked stares with Patel. The eunuch's eyes were steady, neither angry nor malicious. He smiled, as if her rebellion was a passing fancy and she would be taken, one way or another.

Patel leaned forward and stroked her hair. "I will have Maya prepare you. I will tell her to put your hair up, I think, bound with a single pin. Your hair falls so pretty, Orchid." He turned and left.

Jasmine sat on her mattress and weighed her chances of escaping if she ran away immediately. Not good. She needed more time to put a plan together, but how? Maya entered minutes later with a tray. She gave Jasmine a thin golden chain to wear around her waist, golden ankle bracelet, and a silken white choker. Jasmine considered and rejected a dozen half-formed ideas while Maya applied makeup to her eyes, rouged her cheeks and nipples, perfumed her body, and painted on her lips. Next were the candelabra-like earrings with diamonds that struck little bells when her head moved. Her thoughts raced, but no solutions appeared. Her hair was arranged in an elegant twist atop her head, fixed with an ivory pin. Finally, a white veil was fastened around her face.

Jasmine now wore a gauzy white robe that may as well have been nothing. The only article of substance was a pair of panties that would make a stripper blush. And of course, they were white. Maya painted her nails scarlet. When Maya finished, she held up a mirror. Jasmine didn't recognize herself. A mask looked back at her, one that blinked and licked its lips when she did. For the first time in years, she thought she looked pretty, beautiful even. It made her sick. There had to be a way out.

She glanced down at the tray and saw something glint under the mirror.

"Maya, I need the lotion for my hands. I left it in the bath. Could you get it for me?"

Maya stared at her, unblinking. "I would hate to get this wet or smear the makeup or anything," Jasmine said.

Maya stared at Jasmine for many seconds, then down at the white garments. Maya's lips pressed together as if in concentration, then she turned and left the room. Jasmine grabbed the straight razor from the tray and ran as silently down the hall as she could. She ducked into a room assigned to one of the hookah girls. Maybe five minutes before they'd find her, she figured, gotta make it count. She raised the razor with shaking hands.

JASMINE'S HEAD snapped from side to side as Patel's hand fell over and over.

"What have you done, you stupid cow?" he said in a high screech that would have been funny if she wasn't tasting her own blood. Patel reached to the floor and brought up a fistful of her severed hair. He shook it as if he could wring the life from it.

"This is how you repay the generosity of the Caliph, who has fed and clothed you?" he said.

Jasmine spat in his face and grinned. She forced bloody spittle through her teeth for added effect. Her head snapped sideways, the sting of his hand lagging a split second behind the impact. Patel closed his fist, and Jasmine braced for the beating. Patel stood there, jaw set, nostrils flared. He brought the fist down, and Jasmine closed her eyes. The blow never landed. She opened her eyes and saw knuckles a fraction of an inch from her eye.

The fist dropped. Patel closed his eyes and took in several deep breaths. When he looked at her, calm had returned to his voice. "I shall inform the Caliph that it is the time of your cycle, and are therefore unavailable tonight. Do not think this is over, Orchid." He turned and left her.

She lay down, the jewelry at her ankles and wrists jangling. Her head felt cold and a little funny. In some places, it burned where she had nicked her scalp. She was bruised and weary, but she closed her eyes and slept happy.

Cally was there when she woke up, sitting at the edge of the mattress. Patel had Jasmine confined to her room, enforced by a chain running from her wrist to a ring set in the wall.

"You never fuck up just a little, do you?" Cally said. "It's always gonna blow up in some big way."

Jasmine stretched, giving her chain a little shake. "Maybe. I'm surprised you're here."

Cally reached out and stroked Jasmine's scalp. "I had to see what all the fuss was about. Frankly, I think you could have done better. Next time make it a Mohawk."

Jasmine laughed. "Oh? And why's that?"

"Fuck 'em, that's why. Make 'em decide whether to make you walk around all punked out or make the call to shave it off. Never give 'em a break."

"That's funny, I thought you were going native," Jasmine said.

"I'm just saying, you know? I found a good gig here."

"I beg to differ."

"Then enjoy your shaved head. But it's gonna get you in trouble; give you god-awful jewelry." She fingered the manacle. "You know?"

"So I should just roll over and think of England, while some fat slob pumps away on me every night?"

Cally rolled her eyes. "You just won't understand. You want me to say you're tough? Fine, you're tough. But you're no survivor. You're just as dead for standing up as for running."

"So you're going to cower in this cage for the rest of your life."

"Don't know," Cally said. "I'll ride this out until I think I can get something better."

"I can't believe the Caliph is your new dream guy. What about finding Ryan?"

Cally's face clouded. "Just before the party ended in the Badlands, Ryan awoke one night and said he had to go away for a bit and not to tell anyone. Told me not to worry. No one saw him for three weeks. Then one day, he shows up, looking like complete shit, but with this big smile on his face. 'I fixed it, Cally,' he said, 'Now no one will die from hunger anymore.' It wasn't what he intended, Jas. He felt awful about it."

Jasmine's stomach twisted.

"The deaders?"

Cally nodded. "They started showing up a week later."

"That idiot. And then he left."

Cally shook her head. "No, you don't understand. He was only trying to help—is still trying to help. He's going to come back and fix all this. He told me so."

"He left you, Cally. He left everyone behind."

"No, honey, I know him. I'm as much a part of his life as he is of mine. He'll come back. I don't need to find him, I just need to stay safe until he finds me."

Jasmine kept her mouth shut, though she wanted to scream at the woman. Cally leaned in close and whispered in her ear. "You need to stay alive, Jas. Everything else can wait, okay?" Cally pulled back and held Jasmine's face with both hands. "Okay?"

Jasmine stared back. All Cally wanted was her agreement. Just a little okay or a nod and everything would be fine between them. It would be so easy to lie and make her happy. Jasmine looked away. She could feel the tremors in Cally's hands as she bent down and touched her lips to Jasmine's head.

"Bye then, Jas," she said. "Maybe see you in the next one, huh?"

Jasmine glanced back. Cally's face seemed twisted, fighting between a frown and a stiff upper lip. Her blue eyes were glassing over. Jasmine looked away to the wall. Cally got up and left, her quick steps fading. Jasmine thought she was headed for the hookah room, which seemed like a bad idea, but there wasn't a great deal Jasmine could do about it in her present condition.

She wanted to cry for Cally, which was a real riot, she thought, for someone just punched out by a eunuch. But she couldn't afford tears right now. If Patel decided to check on her, he couldn't see her crying. She couldn't afford to show weakness. She wasn't as pretty or curvy as the others, and she sure as hell wasn't going to learn how to be a good lay. She could see it if Cally couldn't: once her virginity was gone, she would no longer be needed. Maybe Cally would forgive her sometime later...maybe.

~

Fighting was harder than she thought.

Patel came to her each day with the needles. He murmured how she was to act and punctuated each bullet point with a needle in a nerve center that sent her convulsing on the mattress or straining against the chains. He kept her awake, half starved. The only thing keeping her going was the little flame she kept alive in her head, shut well away in her mind and fed with the anger and pain from the eunuch's ministrations. He was turning her into an animal, something less than human, she realized in the breaks between sessions. She wondered what kind of gardener twists his flowers into weeds.

Cally never visited.

Jasmine was breaking down. She knew that. She felt herself nodding to Patel's whispers, earning fifteen minutes more sleep after each session. It was Patel's chief coin, the granting of sleep. Food was another, though less effective. Each session seemed timeless, the breaks shorter and shorter. Had the week gone by already? Maybe Patel had convinced the Caliph that he should wait another week before calling her to his bed, maybe another month. She couldn't hold out that long.

When she began answering Patel, she got a whole half hour's rest and a few grapes. When she could recite his list, the needles stopped. When she could perform those acts on a wooden surrogate that wouldn't spoil her, or mime those acts that would, she was given a whole two hours of rest. It felt glorious.

He came to her for one last session, the needles in one hand, a cloth in the other. He bathed her, dried her, and released the shackles. Maya brought in the white garments, and Jasmine quickly put them on. She fastened the jewelry, held still for the makeup, and finally, for the wig Patel placed on her, securing it with some kind of glue. He held out a glass of water, and she drank it. It was sweet, with a tang of mint and something else she couldn't quite place. It made her body warm and her skin prickle.

If she pleased the Caliph, she would get a whole night's sleep. What luxury, she thought. It made her woozy just thinking about it. Maya reached out and steadied her. Jasmine thanked her, though Maya didn't respond. Bitch never did. Though maybe it was because Jasmine's tongue seemed to be thicker than usual. Maybe it was dry.

She asked for more water.

"Just a little more, Orchid," Patel said.

Orchid, that was her. She liked orchids. Always had. She said as much to Patel, who smiled at her. She smiled back, even though Patel's smile seemed off, like he was on the other side of a fisheye lens, but it was kinda funny too. She stifled a giggle as his nose grew and shrank when he planted a kiss on her forehead.

"Let us go my little Orchid."

15

The hallways blurred with wild colors and people who melted in her peripheral vision. She took her steps carefully and leaned on Patel for support. He smelled of the hookah room and cucumbers, which seemed comforting somehow.

They came to a set of red lacquered doors with two black iron rings for handles. Patel knocked three times, each rap like a piece of chalk breaking. The door opened, and a Japanese man opened it. Patel spoke to him, and he glanced once Jasmine's way. His face twisted as he looked at her, and she felt shivers down her back. His hand went to a sword at his waist. Patel exclaimed something in his high voice and placed himself between her and the swordsman.

They argued with each other in that language she didn't understand. Their argument seemed to echo in her head, and she wished she could cover her ears. Why were they so loud? Her mind failed her, like it was fuzzy, useless as a beached whale. Whales. She had never gone whale watching. She thought about that until the yelling stopped.

"We may go now, Orchid," Patel said, snapping her out of it.

"What were you and the angry man talking about?"

"Kikuchiyo is out of sorts tonight, little flower, nothing more."

As they passed, the swordsman turned and stared. His forehead distorted as she passed so that it seemed like his whole face had become two turned-down eyebrows over furious eyes.

Patel ushered her through a short hallway into a room built around a massive circular bed. It rose from the floor like an altar, large enough to accommodate ten people without crowding. She approached it. The sheets were crimson, smooth to the touch. She ran a fingernail across it, a whisper tracing a red stream.

"Do not disappoint me, Orchid," Patel said. He closed the door.

She should feel something, she thought. She remembered having been scared of coming to this place once but now it seemed familiar. Maybe because it smelled like the hookah room, sweet and musky at the same time. She ran her hands over the sheets, the smooth texture tempting her to lie down. A single lamp set over the bed lit the room through layers of red gauze, turning her skin pink. She felt warm again; she looked around for something to drink.

A man stood behind her, looking at her. His image wavered in her vision, but by now she had gotten used to it. What was she supposed to do again? Greet him?

"My Caliph?" she said.

He nodded. He had thinning gray hair, dark skin, and a round face. He wore a white garment too formal to be called a robe, but too casual to be called a suit either. He held out his hands to her, and she crossed the room to him, picking her steps so she wouldn't fall as the room tilted around her. His ringed fingers took her hands, turning them over. He rubbed at her palms with his thumbs, and grunted when he found the cut on her thumb, almost too faint to see.

She looked up at him, and his angry eyes made her feel small. She dropped her gaze, and something inside her head began whispering, calling for her attention, but it was a small thing so she ignored it. The Caliph left her and went to the bed. She thought he had brought out a towel, but as he unfurled it she realized it was a rectangle of white silk. He flung it out and it slowly descended to the bed's center.

"Orchid." She went to him. He undid the wig's trusses, throwing the ivory pin to the bed, and letting it fall around her face. He ran is fingers through it, rubbing the strands between a forefinger and thumb. Then he reached out and removed her robe. His eyes played over her then he turned and opened a bottle sitting on the sideboard behind him. He poured clear oil into a cupped palm. His head tilted back and he drew in a great breath as he rubbed the oil on his hands. He reached out and spread the oil down her shoulders, arms, and back. The whispering thing in her head grew louder but no more understandable. His fingertips traced out her collarbone, breasts, and navel. For a moment, she could almost hear the angry voice but she gasped as the Caliph pinched a nipple and lost her concentration.

He unloosened his sash and the robe fell open, revealing a soft body full of rolls. The voice in her head became angry and she hesitated, but Patel's instructions had been very clear. She ran her lips down the Caliph's chest and belly. Her hand fell to his crotch, and she began massaging him, feeling his member stirring. It wasn't pleasant, but no worse than the hookah room. No worse than Patel's needles. Whenever she thought of stopping, the phantom memory of the needles kept her going.

The voice in her head became a gibbering rush she still couldn't make sense of. She felt confused and couldn't remember what Patel had told her. The Caliph's hands pulled once more at her wig and she felt it tear from her scalp. It should have hurt more than it did, but the pain felt far away. He roared something she couldn't understand, and the wig flew across the room.

He picked her up by her arms and threw her belly-down onto the bed. Fabric ripped across her hips, and a heavy weight fell on her. She felt something wet slip between her thighs. She couldn't breathe. She stretched out and tried to move forward to get some air. The Caliph's hand pinned her by a shoulder, but as he pushed himself forward his bulk lifted up enough for her lungs to fill.

A jagged pain ran through her and she screamed. Her vision wavered and the weight lifted. She was turned over and he stared at her with hunger and greed. Then the suffocating warmth and numbness vanished and the angry jibbering in her head coalesced into thought as the blood trickled down her thigh and made her mind whole again. She was Jasmine once more.

She scowled at the Caliph. He just smiled back at her. She moved to get away, but his hands pinned hers to the bed. She shouted and thrashed, but he continued to leer and slowly lowered himself to her. She looked up at him and spat. He rubbed the spittle off against his shoulder and made to thrust himself into her once more.

She fought, betrayed by a body already too weak to throw him off. She kicked at his bulk, only managing glancing blows from her awkward position. Caliph's face loomed closer and in a moment, recognized him – the jawline, the nose, the set of the eyes. The features obscured by age and fat, the skin color all wrong, but the resemblance was undeniable...her brother's face.

"No," she said and felt as if her whole body was being dipped in tar. "Ryan, no, stop it," she said, and he paused, closing his eyes. She stretched her fingers toward the edge of the bed, trying to get some leverage to topple him, knowing it was futile. Her fingertips brushed against something round and smooth. She looked over and found the ivory chopstick-like pin just beyond reach.

"Ryan," she pleaded. The Caliph opened his eyes and looked down, a look of shock coming over his face. The Caliph's body seemed to shrink into itself, the swarthy color fading to a lighter yellowish hue. Gray balding hair gave way to thick black. The Ryan she remembered looked down at her.

"Jas?" he said, and he looked at his groin, smeared with blood. White cloth soaked red, blood covering her thighs. "No…" He pushed himself away.

"Why?" Jasmine said. Tears stung her eyes. Ryan looked from himself to Jasmine and shook his head from side to side.

"No, not real, not real," he said, covering his eyes. "Wake up, wake up, wake up!" He pulled at his hair with both hands, and his eyes rolled back into his head. His body started changing. His skin darkened and aged, his belly swelled, his hair went gray. Jasmine reached out to the ivory pin. When she looked back, the Caliph stared back at her with greedy eyes, all traces of her brother now gone. He lunged at her.

Jasmine swung, driving the pin into the Caliph's ear. He roared and grabbed at her wrist as blood came flowing down her fingers. Jasmine worked the pin around, sending the Caliph into spasms and howling. He slapped at her arms, weakly. Jasmine probed with the pin and drove it in further. The Caliph gasped and screamed soundlessly while his whole body twitched and shivered. Jasmine drove it in another half inch, and his eyes glazed over. For a few heartbeats they stayed there, frozen. Then the Caliph fell.

Jasmine pulled herself free of the body and crawled off the bed onto the floor. Her body shook uncontrollably, and she used her remaining strength to curl into a ball.

She was too tired. Too numb. She felt hollow, sick, filthy. It would be a blessing to be killed when they found her. She had earned the right, hadn't she? Hadn't she? And if she wanted to die, there wasn't anyone around to stop her anymore. Bishop was dead, and Cally had left her. So let's just get it over with.

She lay there for a few more moments, naked and shivering. The black thoughts swirled in her head. She could picture herself lying naked and bloody on the floor, whimpering. She was pathetic. It made her sick to see herself like this.

And yet a part of her still held onto life, refusing to let it go. The same part that kept the little flame going while Patel broke the rest of her. The same part that shouted at the Caliph. The same part that had shaved her head, kissed Bishop, and held onto the beacon tower's ladder instead of jumping. She was still missing something in life and this burning part of her knew death held no answers. Only now with the rest of her mind crumbling could she listen to it.

She held the little flame in her mind to all the black thoughts running though her head. They were slowly consumed one by one until only a single simple truth remained: she was tired of running away from life's disappointments.

"Get up," she said aloud. "No more running."

16

She uncurled herself, got to her hands and knees, and pulled against the bed to get upright. There was an ache between her legs and she pushed the reason for it into a dark closet in her mind. When there was time, she would deal with it. She stumbled over to a cabinet with glass shelves holding cut glass tumblers and several bottles of brown liquor. The mirror behind the bottles gave her glimpses of blood, torn clothing, and a skinny girl who could barely stand. She reached for a bottle and poured herself a glass. She raised it to her lips, stopping short as she considered it being laced with more than just alcohol.

"Damn," she said, throwing the drink at the wall. The liquid ran to the floor and seeped into the carpeting. The fumes hung in the air, making her eyes water.

Jasmine walked around the room, avoiding the corpse, the blood, and the mirrors. She recalled the doorway led back to the Blood Weeper, but the Caliph had entered another way. She searched the room and felt a breeze revealing a second doorway, disguised as a wall panel. The dark passageway behind the panel seemed a better option than facing the angry samurai.

She put one foot into the passage and stopped. Running down a dark hallway into the unknown would be just plain dumb.

"Plan, plan, plan," she said out loud. She looked at herself. A naked blood-soaked harem girl would definitely attract attention.

She rummaged around the bottles on the shelf until she found some water. She wadded up her gauzy robe and washed herself quickly. She then put on the Caliph's pants and robe top, tying and cinching the extra material as best she could with ropes and cords she found in a drawer next to razors, lashes, and oddly-shaped devices that made her shudder when she realized where they were intended to be inserted. She lashed the extra material in place and looked in the mirror, making sure not to look at the thing on the bed. She thought her outfit looked like a white version of the robes the slavers wore; she would find a way to dirty it up later and hope people wouldn't look at her too closely.

"A diversion," she said. She scanned the room, and her eyes settled on the draperies over the bed. The words of her dorm's RA from freshman year popped into her head.

"For God's sake, ladies, don't hang crap from the ceiling like nets or curtains. My first year here, someone almost burned down Wharton Hall because their party decorations were too close to the light bulb."

She stepped onto the bed, taking care not to disturb the body or the blood pools collecting around it. She tried looping a curtain around the overhead light, but the fixture was too far away for her to reach, and covered by a glass plate. She wasn't going to start any fires that way. She leapt down and forced herself to go through the drawers again.

"Think like a survivor," she told herself. The idea helped, and she soon found herself placing folding razors in her makeshift outfit with a coiled whip at her waist. A small iron-studded club with a leather loop at the handle was first washed of dried blood and other fluids, then placed on the opposite hip.

The fourth drawer yielded a few candles and a box of matches.

"Jackpot."

She went about barricading the door, and then doused the room with oil.

≈

ALARMS RANG THROUGH THE DECKS. The hidden passageway split before her. She stopped and looked down two identical hallways. The Caliph would have an escape route one way, but the other? A throne room? A secret way back to the *hareem*? She couldn't know which way led where, or even if it split again somewhere up ahead. A sign on the left indicated the way to the flight deck. The Caliph would have a way to escape quickly, a personal ornithopter, perhaps. The right was unmarked and seemed to lead deeper into the palace, but she couldn't be sure. Fuck it, she thought, she wasn't leaving just yet. Not without Cally. She flipped a mental coin and took the right-hand hallway. She would find Cally. There was just no other option.

Jasmine ran through the passageway and came to a section with metal floor grating and yellow-brown lights. The smell of sandalwood and incense gave way to the tang of metal and something sickly-sweet. The floor vibrated with a deep thrumming. She considered turning back when she heard voices.

"Boost the power, necro, or I'll make sure that when this heap goes down you'll be chained to the boilers."

"Boosting the power can't help us if the fire spreads to the envelope," a familiar voice said. "We need to—"

A muffled thud cut the voice short.

"I told you what to do, necro, do it!"

Jasmine peered around the corner, through an open metal door leading to a catwalk. It ran over a bay containing what looked like a small sun enclosed in a glass tank, surrounded by coffin-shaped boxes stacked five high. At the tank's base, wedged between the boxes, Helgo lay in front of a levered and knobbed panel. A tall, heavyset man with a truncheon stood over him.

Helgo swayed as he rose to his feet and steadied himself against the panel. Behind him, the man shifted from foot to foot and slapped the truncheon against an open palm.

Jasmine crept on a metal catwalk, her slippers making no sound. She walked as if on a tightrope, wary that any sudden shift in weight might make the metal creak. She stopped above Helgo and threw a leg over the railing. Then she gathered a breath, checked her landing, and jumped.

She must have made a noise because the guard looked up a moment before her heels drove through his shoulders. She landed awkwardly, and her head smacked against the decking, sending white chips of light floating before her eyes. Jasmine willed herself to get up, focusing on getting one arm under her, then another. The guard grunted in pain as he tried pushing himself up. His eyes met hers and went wide with a mixture of surprise and raw anger.

Jasmine made it to her feet only to fall down again as the deck seemed to spin around her. The guard smiled and pushed himself to one knee.

Get up, Jas, get up, get up.

The deck still spun as she tried to rise. The guard blurred in her vision. She reached for a knife, and readied herself to strike when a dark shadow jumped on the guard's back. The guard's head slammed to the decking and seemed to bounce in time to a muffled thudding.

Jasmine's vision cleared to see Helgo stepping away, a dark-stained hammer in his hands, the guard's head cracked and leaking blood.

"Nice of you to drop in, girl," Helgo said.

"Captivity hasn't improved your sense of humor."

"Or yours." He nodded to the guard and grinned his black-toothed grin. "Thank you again. Seems I owe you two lives now."

"You can start by helping me find Cally."

"We should leave. The Caliphate is on fire."

"I know. I'm the one that started it."

"I'm not surprised."

"We can leave once we get Cally out of the *hareem*."

"Is that all, sneaking a girl out of the holy-of-holies?" He blew out a short laugh. "Then we better make some help." He moved toward the guard's body and began straightening it out. "Go bring me that toolbox and then give me a hand with this one. We don't have much time."

Helgo dipped his finger in engine grease and painted glyphs and sigils on the overseer's body. He hummed a song in the back of his throat as he worked, waving Jasmine to silence when she was about to ask what he was doing. After humming three songs, both Helgo and the corpse were covered in greasy tattoos. He grunted as he rose and looked about.

"What do you need?" Jasmine said.

"Need a wire about yea thick," Helgo said, making a circle with his thumb and forefinger.

Jasmine cast about the room and found a cable running between a console and one of the machine's outer pods. She held it up, and Helgo shook his head.

"Bigger. That's a baby python. I need its mother."

Jasmine went farther inside the machinery and found a larger cable. She stood and gasped as she caught a glimpse inside the pod. Beneath the translucent glass lay a thin, blackened body. The hair looked like patchwork, frazzled in one place, down to smooth scalp in others. Then it hit her: a deader. She was in an engine room, surrounded by deaders.

"Any luck?" Helgo called out.

"There's one the size of my wrist," she said.

"That'll do. Hang on, I'm coming back with some cutters," Helgo said.

He shuffled toward her, careful not to rub his grease marks against the pod frames.

"They're all deaders, aren't they?"

"Sure are. They're powering the Caliphate, and keeping it aloft, but they're overtaxed. They'll burn out before long, and then the Caliphate becomes a gilded rock."

He twisted a brass plug where the cable met the pod and pulled it free. He measured out about ten feet and snipped it with the cutters.

"So what are you doing?"

"If we're going to get your friend out of the harem, we'll need a weapon. I can't get these deaders decoupled without blowing us all the hell up, so I need to jump start a new one. Here." He handed her the cable's plug end and shuffled back toward the overseer's body, stuffing the cable's severed end into the dead man's mouth.

Jasmine wrinkled her nose at the plug. "We're not..."

"Jump-starting a corpse? Nah. Just plug that in when I give the nod."

Helgo started humming again, a sickening upbeat song that tickled at Jasmine's memory. A song some girl had played over and over again at her birthday party and they were all supposed to learn a choreographed routine that went along with it. Jasmine had never quite gotten the hang of it and always seemed a step behind no matter how many times the birthday girl made her repeat it.

Helgo nodded, and Jasmine plugged the cable into the socket, still trying to remember what the name of the damned song was. She jumped as a blue-white light shot from the corpse's mouth with a sharp crack. The cable skittered along the floor, showering sparks as it bounced. The body convulsed in seizures while Helgo clapped and hopped from foot to foot. The convulsions intensified as Helgo clapped faster until the body jerked its torso upright. The head turned and tracked Helgo's cavorting form with unseeing eyes. Helgo's clapping changed to syncopated triplets, and the overseer's body rocked forward and rose to its feet.

Helgo stopped and let his arms go limp. Jasmine unplugged the cable and blinked blue and green after images from her eyes. The overseer stood still, staring ahead. Jasmine caught her breath, then rounded on Helgo.

"I thought you said—"

Helgo shrugged. "I lied. Do you want to take more time arguing about it or get off this tub?"

Jasmine stared at him for a moment, then said, "Fine." She pointed a finger in his face. "But don't do it again."

"Okay," he said, though it sounded like another lie. "The harem should be this way." Jasmine walked toward the bulkhead door, but Helgo stopped her. "Let him go first," he said, pointing to the former overseer. "They won't stop us if they think he's in charge, and he'll take the first few bullets if they get suspicious."

"Okay," Jasmine said. "What was that song you just hummed?"

Helgo grinned his black-toothed grin. "'Goody Two-Shoes,' Adam Ant."

"Of course. I hated that song."

"Me too. But with deaders, there's no accounting for taste."

THE *HAREEM'S* entry stood unguarded. People rushed past them, arms filled with bright clothing and jewelry. They pushed past Jasmine, Helgo, and the overseer's corpse down the hallway leading to the flight deck.

"Rats can always sense a sinking ship," Helgo said.

When they went inside, Patel and the girls were all gone. The hookah lay in pieces, gold fittings and opium missing, the rest abandoned. Jasmine picked up a large chunk from the remains and stared at the tar-like stains from the drugs.

"It stinks," Helgo said.

"I suppose it does," Jasmine said, dropping the ceramic. Funny how she had gotten used to it. "Where would they have gone?"

"I'd guess the flight deck is the popular place to be right about now."

"Then that's where we'll go to find Cally."

"And a way off, I hope."

17

———

They surveyed the flight deck and palace courtyard from behind a stack of crates. Guards herded the Caliphate into groups in the courtyard by station, with the courtiers closest to the flight deck. The servants and slaves were forced to the back, away from the flight line where ornithopters prepared to launch. There was a sense of unease but not panic despite the smoke billowing from the palace. Jasmine didn't think that would last much longer.

"I don't see Cally," she said.

"Probably have the harem out of sight. Propriety must be maintained, even at times like this," Helgo said.

"I'll go look for her," Jasmine said, pulling a flap of cloth over her mouth and nose. Helgo grabbed her arm.

"No, wait. You can pass for a guard at a distance, but up close they'll spot you for sure."

"You have a better idea?"

Helgo grinned. "This shit is way too orderly. Wait here until I signal, then make your move. I'll meet you and Cally on the lower flight deck, port side."

"What's the signal?"

"Oh, do you really have to ask?" He whistled at the corpse, which put its hand around Helgo's arm and began pulling him across the courtyard. Helgo hung his head and shuffled along behind his puppet, humming a low tune.

Guards turned to look but didn't move to stop them. They walked past the courtiers into a palace hallway.

Jasmine ran her hands over her outfit, fixing the scalpels, knives, and other tools in her makeshift bandoleer to memory. Minutes later, an explosion erupted from the courtyard's far end, shaking the decks. Dirty orange fireballs rose from the windows and roof, merging into a roiling mushroom overhead. Everyone on deck froze for a moment, then began screaming and running in all directions. Jasmine recognized the man in the blue suit, emerging from a crouch and shouting at the guards, forming them into groups and issuing orders.

The guards ran across the courtyard to the flight deck, returning with hoses and buckets. Black smoke poured from the Caliph's palace roof. From her hiding place behind the crates, she watched the courtiers, servants, and slaves merge into a single mass, pressing toward the flight deck, away from the fire. The man in the blue suit stood like a rock in the rapids, directing guards and mob alike.

A fire brigade shot water into blasted-out windows, but it seemed to Jasmine that it wouldn't be enough to stop the blaze. Soon it would be apparent to everyone else and the mob would turn ugly. 'Thopter rotors began whining, and the mob pressed against a line of guards blocking the flight line.

She searched for Cally as the mob and guards jostled before spotting Patel and several guards carrying out the harem women from a door billowing oily smoke. Most of the girls flopped to the ground or slumped into a heap and looked at the chaos around them with dazed and frightened looks. One of them had blonde hair.

Jasmine darted from her hiding place and fell into line behind a group of guards carrying buckets. If any thought her outfit strange, it was soon forgotten as they fought through the mob. Voices, arms, legs, and hands formed a wall slowing Jasmine's pace to a crawl. Halfway across the courtyard, the mob thinned, and she peeled off toward the harem girls. A few courtiers and servants had formed a rough circle around the girls, perhaps thinking it was the safest place to be in the chaos. Patel kept the area clear, glowering at anyone coming within ten feet of his charges.

Jasmine reached to her belt and pulled out a thin razor. There were three layers of people between her and Patel. The eunuch was turned away, yelling at some servant that had breached the sacred boundary of the *hareem's* new location. Jasmine sprinted.

As she passed the first layer, people turned to look. She pumped her legs harder, shouldering through those in the second layer. At the final layer, old serving women with pocked faces and hard eyes gave way to her. Patel seemed to sense her approach and his head turned.

She didn't think. Two steps away, their eyes met. She saw the recognition pass over his face. He spun, bringing his arms up as the razor lashed out. His forearms smashed into hers, but too late. A ribbon of red flew from Patel's neck, spraying her face. The razor clattered to the ground as her arms went numb.

His hands went to his neck as he retreated. Blood spurted through his fingers and began showering the stunned crowd. A cry went out, and the innermost layers of the crowd began running away with blood on their faces. Patel came at her with one red-soaked hand on his neck, another reaching for her. Jasmine kicked, and he caught her ankle in a vice-like grip. Jasmine kicked several times more, trying to get free, but his grip held. He pulled her toward him, rage in his eyes. His other hand reached for her throat, heedless of his wound. Together they fell.

His hand, slick with blood, batted hers away and fastened on her neck. Jasmine lashed out as he released her ankle and clamped both hands to her throat. Her foot slammed into his groin, making him grunt, but his grip held. As her vision went black at the edges, Patel brought his face close to hers.

"We die together, Orchid."

She reached up, and her thumb found his eye. He cried out, and his grip slackened just enough for her to gasp. His strength returned but was already fading. The fountain spraying from his neck pulsed weaker each time. By the time the air in her lungs began getting stale, Patel's hand slid from her neck and he fell to the ground.

18

J asmine rolled to her feet. The crowd had worked itself into a full panic, running in all directions. The man in the blue suit shouted and pointed, but they paid him no heed. Guards broke off from firefighting to reinforce the line holding the mob back from the flight deck.

Jasmine walked to Cally, huddled in a mass of harem girls who were too drugged to stand. Jasmine held out her hand. Cally shook her head and turned to bury her face into the stomach another harem girl.

"Cally, it's me, Jasmine," she said. She took the cloth off her head. "Really, look at me."

Cally looked back, and while she still looked scared, seemed to recognize her.

"Come on, we're getting out of here." She held her hand out to Cally. Cally reached tentatively, and Jasmine pulled her from the pile of drugged flesh. Cally held a small bundle close to her chest. Jasmine put a hand on it, and Cally snatched it away.

"We don't have time for this. You gotta come with me." Cally half turned and took a step in Jasmine's direction. Jasmine caught Cally's free arm as the woman swayed and nearly tripped over her own feet. "Stay with me, girl." She put herself under Cally's shoulder and turned them toward the 'thopter pads.

The crowd surged around them and Jasmine felt herself and Cally being picked up like flotsam on an ocean wave. Jasmine kept her legs moving, pushed from behind, afraid to stop or be trampled. Cally weighed heavily on her right and was in constant danger of pulling them under.

She managed to get herself and Cally to the edge of the mob as it broke through the guards and surged onto the flight deck. People jostled and rocked the craft from side to side, pleading for escape as pilots and crew tried to wave them off. Jasmine saw the cockpit window on one 'thopter open and a man scramble toward it, stepping on and over the shoulders of others. He shrieked with joy just before a pistol cracked and his head split open. The throng drew back for a moment, staring at the fallen man. 'Thopters began lifting, their engines kicking up dust. Cockpit windows and cargo doors began sprouting weapons.

A shout went up, and people began climbing on the 'thopters. Weapons fired and bodies fell, but the mob surged. Several craft began clawing into the air as pilots fought with their controls. Then one 'thopter, people clinging to its body like ants attacking a beetle, dipped one wing and tumbled over the Caliphate's edge.

A shudder ran through the mob as a wedge of guards forced their way to the ornithopters, smashing and crushing any who got in their way. The man in the blue suit anchored the wedge's middle, a silver pistol in his hand. The mob pushed back, and the flight deck descended into a melee.

Jasmine kept to the edges, looking for a way to the lower flight deck. She noticed one of the Caliph's raiders emerge from the palace and dash around the edges of the fighting to disappear down a flight of stairs. Did the stairs lead to the lower flight deck, port side? Was port left or right? She'd figure it out later.

"Come on, Cally, we're going down those stairs."

Jasmine dragged Cally across the decking, hoping the fighting would stay focused around the 'thopters. A muffled, crunching sound came from the palace and another smoke plume billowed into the air with a column of flame licking after it. The deck tilted and Jasmine's legs screamed as she pulled Cally to the stairs, which turned out to be a glorified metal ladder. Jasmine turned to Cally and held the woman's face between her hands.

"Cally, you've got to move on your own now and follow me. Can you do that?"

Cally's eyes wandered from side to side, not focusing. "Yeah," she said, "follow you."

Jasmine let the woman go. Cally wavered for a few moments but kept her balance with the handrail's help.

"Okay, wait here a second," Jasmine said.

Jasmine half-climbed, half-slipped down the stairwell, getting just enough grip from the chipped red paint on the steel handrails to keep control. She was on some kind of observation deck, with a skinny railing between her and open sky. It ran the length of the ornithopter deck above, with ladders leading to other sections. Flames raged to her left, crawling across the rear of the Caliphate, now cutting off the palace entirely. Jasmine leaned over the railing and saw the flames had engulfed not only the upper deck, but were working their way to the house-sized props, still turning and pushing the ship forward.

The wailing and screaming of those trapped in the palace cut through the shouts and gunfire above. One courtier jumped from a window and fell spread-eagled. Another man, already on fire, turned and twisted in the air, leaving a smoke trail in his wake.

Jasmine turned her eyes away, and forced herself to look farther over the side. Just below, small ornithopters hung from the ship's steel skeleton. The raider she had seen earlier jumped into a 'thopter through the open cockpit and reached overhead to work a lever. The 'thopter fell away from the ship, arcing away from the Caliphate as the craft's engines started.

"Just a bit farther, Cally," Jasmine called up to her. The woman climbed down the ladder with agonizing slowness, missing a few steps along the way, but she made it down. Jasmine put herself under Cally's arm once more and pulled her to the next stairway.

They found their way down by taking any ladder going down and any passage leading left. For once fortune smiled on them and the passageways were clear of both people and smoke. Cally began standing on her own, leaving Jasmine free to scout ahead at each intersection. She hoped Cally would snap out of it soon, but there wasn't time to hold her hand just now.

They stepped off the last ladder onto the lower flight deck, a platform with metal grating that seemed less a deck and more like steel fingers stretching across open sky. However many 'thopters had been stored here, she didn't know. All she did know was there was just one left. Winds whipped at her headdress and howled into her ears as Jasmine clawed her way to the dagger-like ornithopter sitting in its cradle. The Caliphate's pitch had worsened, and she would soon be forced to climb on hands and knees. Where was Helgo?

"I need you to climb with me, Cally, on your own. Can you do it?" Cally's eyes focused, and the blonde woman thrust out her bundle to Jasmine. It was lighter than Jasmine would have guessed, given how Cally had struggled with it. A package wrapped in gauzy blue fabric, no heavier than a change of clothes, no larger than a basketball.

"Take this for me, Jas," she said, "Just leave me here. I'm tired."

"No." She looked into Cally's eyes and smiled. "You're a lousy friend, but you're all I have."

"It's okay, I don't mind. Ryan will just make another me."

Jasmine couldn't think. How had Cally known she wasn't…*Wasn't what, Jas? Real?* How long had Cally known, waiting for her Ryan in the middle of hell, in all probability forgotten and replaced?

"We've always known, Jas. We tend to live longer if we don't let on."

Jasmine threw her arms around Cally and squeezed.

"I don't want another Cally," she whispered into her friend's ear. "You're the Cally worth saving."

Cally's arms folded around her, and she nodded.

"Okay," Cally said.

"We need to go. Keep your eyes on me; don't look down."

"I can make it from here." Cally managed a weak smile.

Jasmine nodded and pushed herself forward, cradling the bundle in one arm. She slid into the cockpit and stared at the controls. There was very little to it, a few dials, buttons, and a stick jutting up from between two pedals on the floor. She didn't recognize anything.

"Shit. Cally, hurry up!" She wedged Cally's bundle under the seat and strapped herself in.

Cally had almost made it to the 'thopter, eyes locked forward, her face screwed up in concentration, determined not to look down. The deck's pitch forced her to take small steps, but she was making progress. Jasmine hoped Helgo would show up before she was forced to launch.

She turned back to the control panel. One of these buttons had to start the engines, she thought. She pressed at them one by one until the craft's engine whined and sent a shudder through the airframe before cutting out. She pressed the button and held it in. The engine whined, building up in pitch until it caught and sent the craft surging forward into its docking cradle. Metal crunched above her and sent vibrations through her that made her stomach clench. She looked up at a twisted latch marked RELEASE.

"Stupid, stupid," she said to herself, and shut down the engines. "Cally!" she yelled, while she pulled back on a lever she guessed was the throttle.

"Coming, Jas, I—"

Jasmine looked up to see Cally just a few feet away. She was looking down with a surprised look at the sharpened steel sprouting from under her left breast. She looked up at Jasmine with an almost apologetic look and fell to the deck. Kikuchiyo stood behind her in a red and black kimono with strands of unkempt hair escaping his topknot and streaming in the wind. He looked down at Cally's body and his face clouded. The flesh in his face flowed and reformed. A wail escaped from the samurai and when he looked up it was with Ryan's face, contorted with anguish and tears spilling from his eyes.

"I'm sorry, Jas, I didn't mean to hurt her — hurt you. I can't control it anymore, they've taken over." He clutched at his face. His skin bubbled as his tears turned pink.

"Help me."

Before Jasmine could speak, his hands dropped and Kikuchiyo's bloody visage scowled back at her. With a grunt, he removed his sword from Cally's body snapped the tip up to point at Jasmine's eyes. A blood droplet hit her in the face.

"You," he said, "We did not ask you here. He does not need you; we do not need you." He stepped forward, kicking Cally's body to the side.

Jasmine watched Cally's body drop into the sky. Blonde hair came free, framing Cally's face as the body tumbled. Kikuchiyo's grunt brought Jasmine to her senses. She reached up and worked at the lever to release the 'thopter. It moved halfway and then stopped. The 'thopter swung back and forth as metal screamed on metal. She pumped her arm forward and back, but the latch was stuck, jammed. The samurai stood next to the 'thopter now, the sword point only a few feet from her face. He grimaced and brought his arm back to strike. Jasmine heard singing, and someone grabbed at the Blood Weeper from behind.

The sword halted in mid-air. Kikuchiyo snarled and backhanded the overseer's corpse. The corpse's head rocked backward, but its grip on the samurai's sword arm remained. The overseer backed up, pulling the samurai with him step by step, away from the ornithopter. As the two struggled, a black form slid beneath their legs. Helgo climbed into the ornithopter, gesturing Jasmine to the back as he slid into the pilot's position. He hummed a song and cast glances over his shoulder at the struggling pair.

"What—" Jasmine said, but was cut off by a quick shake of Helgo's head.

He pointed to a handle above their heads and made a breaking motion with his hands. She nodded and started working at the handle. Helgo violently shook his head and patted the air with both hands. He hooked a thumb at himself and then pointed at the ornithopter's engines. Jasmine nodded. She would wait for Helgo to start the engines. Kikuchiyo shouted and Helgo's eyes went wide.

His control had slipped, as had the corpse's grip on the samurai. The Blood Weeper's eyes streamed crimson and his blade lodged deep in the overseer's chest. The corpse's arms scrabbled feebly to regain a hold. Kikuchiyo freed the blade and as the corpse took a step closer, whipped the sword down, severing an arm. Helgo's humming changed pitch, and the overseer lunged for the samurai's head. Dead fingers closed around his greasy topknot and jerked the samurai closer. Their heads cracked together, the samurai grunting at the impact. The deader showed no response except to jerk the samurai's head again into its own, over and over again.

The ornithopter's engines caught, turbines spinning, a low whine pitching up to a howl. The craft shuddered in its cradle. Helgo turned to look over his shoulder at her and nodded. Jasmine reached for the handle. Something flew past her, and Helgo stopped humming. The overseer's headless corpse hit the catwalk's railing, then fell and tumbled overboard. Jasmine looked over her shoulder as Kikuchiyo rolled to his feet, clearing his sword, bringing its tip to aim right at her eyes. He stepped forward.

"You bring nothing but ruin," he said, bringing the sword up overhead. Helgo yelled at her. The sword fell.

One of the main engines exploded and the whole Caliphate lurched. The samurai stumbled and fell. The sword buried its point in the cradle's latch. Another explosion, this one sending a concussion wave that squeezed Jasmine's organs. A metallic ping rang out overhead like a cracked bell. She tried to get her lungs working as the 'thopter swung back and forth. Kikuchiyo, farther down the deck, struggled to his feet. He brought up a broken sword and looked along its edge. His face reddened, and he let out a roar. Jasmine glanced up and found the sword's tip jammed in the 'thopter cradle's latch.

She reached up and worked at the handle once more, timing her pulls with the swaying ornithopter. The lever gave just a bit each time at the apex of the 'thopter's upswing. The Blood Weeper fought his way back up the pitched decking, a fierce yell punctuating each step and handhold.

One more swing, she thought, but the Blood Weeper arrived just as the 'thopter swung back. He snarled at her. Jasmine reached to her robe and drew a razor. It was pitiful compared to the sword, a mere inch of naked blade against the Weeper's *katana*. She brought her arm down as the 'thopter shifted forward. Her wrist snapped and the razor spun toward the samurai.

Time slowed down for Jasmine, and she could see everything in crystal clarity. She felt her heart thump once in her chest, her back pressing into the 'thopter's seat as it came forward. The razor completed one lazy turn and flew edge-on at the samurai's face. His sword came up as the 'thopter's swing reached its apex. The sword's jagged end pushed the razor away, sending it tumbling. Jasmine's arm pushed the lever. The latch opened and the *katana's* broken tip fell to her feet. The Blood Weeper's blade reached for her.

With scream of steel on steel, the 'thopter fell free. The sword passed over her.

Jasmine fell away from the Caliphate, the Weeper's bloody face framed by greasy black hair, his screams mingling with the 'thopter's engine whine. When the Weeper's scream ended, he glared at her for a moment longer and turned away, disappearing into the belly of the floating palace. Thick black clouds streamed from the Caliphate, 'thopters lifted off from its decks, like flies from a carcass. Smaller forms fell through the air.

Helgo rolled the craft upside down and plunged toward the ground.

"Hey!" Jasmine said. Her head felt suddenly heavier, and her body pressed back into the seat.

"Time to bug the hell out of this party," Helgo said. "Let's hope they're all too busy to notice us and don't follow."

Helgo twisted the ornithopter around into a canyon and leveled off closer to the ground than Jasmine considered safe. She twisted around and saw the Caliphate had become a black smudge at the head of a long, thin stream of smoke.

"Follow us where?" she said.

"Paradise City."

"Then what?"

"You tell me."

Jasmine slumped back in the seat and watched the dead scrub blur by. She closed her eyes and saw a naked and bloody Caliph kneeling over her with Ryan's face. A sword sticking through Cally's chest, a sword held by her brother. Cally's body dropping through the clouds. A burning Biscayne. The Caliph, the Blood Weeper, Ryan. The brother who created heaven and ran away when it became hell. The brother who turned everything he touched into shit. The brother who ruined her old life and was doing it to her again. It had to stop. They had to find a better heaven than this, one run by a proper God. She knew then what she had to do. She would help him.

"We find Ryan," she said.

She would find him, and she would kill him.

BONUS MATERIALS

But wait, there's more!

If you made it this far, I'm guessing you enjoyed this trip into the Badlands (that, or you're a completist, which I totally respect). To continue exploring the mysterious Badlands, get the next book right now.

Get Badlands Cursed

Get The Good Stuff!

Would you like to know more about deaders and necros? If you sign up for the mailing list I'll send you a free ebook you can't get anywhere else, Black Betty: A Badlands Story, featuring your favorite necrosonic engineer, Helgo.

Building a relationship with my readers and talking about stories are two of my favorite things about writing. I occasionally send out updates on new releases, special offers, and other tasty bits relating to the series I'm writing.

Sign up at WadePeterson.com

If you just want to do the simplest thing

If all that is too much but you enjoyed my book, please consider leaving a review. Reviews are the lifeblood of indie books like this and I would consider it a personal favor — just a quick star rating with a sentence or two can make a huge difference in convincing others to give this book a try.

I am on a quest to get 100 reviews of this book and I can only do it with your help.

Of course I'll leave a review!

ABOUT THE AUTHOR

Wade Peterson is a man. He's pretty sure he is, anyway. When they separated the boys and girls in the fourth grade to watch the filmstrip on puberty, they put him with the boys. The voice on the filmstrip said Wade would become a man. Then a bunch of stuff happened, and he wrote the book you just read. If any part of this book is confusing, blame it on the fourth grade.

Click on the icons below to follow Wade on social media for updates, fun pictures, and the occasional cat video. Of course the best stuff is at wadepeterson.com (just saying).

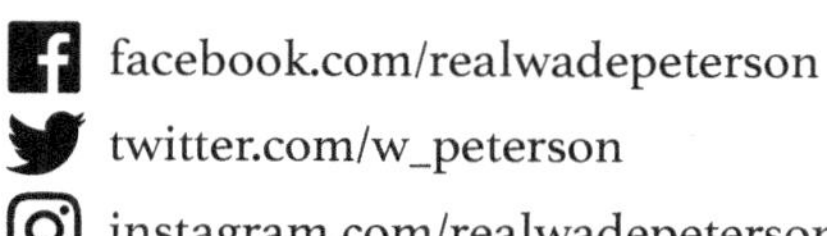

facebook.com/realwadepeterson

twitter.com/w_peterson

instagram.com/realwadepeterson